Halo

A Sequel in *The Light Book Series*

GAIL PATE

PAGE PUBLISHING, INC.
Conneaut Lake, PA

First originally published by Page Publishing 2019

ISBN 978-1-64628-418-4 (pbk)
ISBN 978-1-64628-420-7 (hc)
ISBN 978-1-64628-419-1 (digital)

Printed in the United States of America

For all of us who refuse to let the mistakes we make in this life define our stories…

"Keep looking to the stars and never give up on your dreams."

I thought of Ben's words as I pulled the letter from my pocket. I held on to the single piece of paper where…somehow, within the words written there…contained a part of my heart. I let the curtain fall back into place, walked over, and took the box out of my bag and set it on the stand by the bed. I opened the lid and placed the letter inside. Gently running my finger across the top…

"But how could you ever find me here?"

Part One

Chapter One

I tried to count the fence posts as we drove along the narrow blacktop road leading to my stepdad's family ranch. One, two, three, four…until they began to run together, and I would have to start all over again.

There was not much else to look at since we had left the airport in our rental car; just open land for miles, with two mountain ranges in the distance. *Who would want to live here?* I asked myself as I again lost count of the posts.

"You're awfully quiet, Luvy. I know it's not the beach, but promise me you'll try to have a good time and not be too hard on your mom," Aunt Abby said, looking ahead as the farmhouse came into view.

I glanced over at her as we turned onto the gravel lane lined with pine trees. She gave me that smile—a smile that always made me feel better, then she reached over and gently patted my leg.

"It'll be all right." She winked.

"If you say so," I managed to say under my breath. But I knew it would not be all right. How could it? I was not the same…everything had changed since our trip to the beach house last spring, or at least it had for me.

Everyone else seemed to be going about their lives as if nothing had happened. No one talked about it; no one wanted me to talk about it. They were always changing the subject or saying things like *Things happen for a reason. Maybe it was better this way.* They couldn't seem to understand that I didn't want it to be behind me. I couldn't forget about what happened, and I would not just forget about Ben.

Every time I looked into the mirror, I saw his face. Every time I got into the shower, I remembered the warmth of his kiss. At night when I went to sleep, I heard his voice in my dreams…only to wake and realize that it was only just a dream. But for now, it was all I had to hold on to. It was all I had to hold on to him.

It had been over a year since I had been with him on the beach that morning. *I will find you,* he had said. It was a promise he had made to me and one that I clung to. It was the one thing that had gotten me through the past months. It felt like something was missing…as if I left a part of me there somehow. A sadness that I couldn't quite shake.

I had gone through the motions of school, my junior year, withdrawing from everyone, my dad, my friends, not going to the prom, quitting the swim team. I would never be able to get in the pool again…how could I?

You know we depend on you, you are one of our best swimmers, Coach Allison had pleaded. I was becoming accustomed to letting people down.

The only thing that I could focus on was Ben, knowing that Aunt Abby and I would be going back to the beach house this summer. He would be there, he had to be…it was the place that had brought us together. *Fate*, he had called it. It was the place where our souls had connected. That had to be why I had not heard from him; he was there waiting for me.

We had not gone back to the beach house last summer, or on spring break like we always did. Uncle John was still concerned about the reports of the water being contaminated. *Maybe in the summer*, he had said.

I knew that was not the issue at all. That was the least of the concerns as to what had happened in the waters off the coast. *If they only knew*, I often thought, and how I wished I could tell them.

I thought I would die…waiting. Just like everything else, I had no control in my life…as if it was not even my own. And now, we were not in South Carolina, we were here in this godforsaken land. My mom had somehow convinced her to come here instead.

It'll be good for us, Luvy. A change of scenery is good once in a while. The beach house and the ocean will always be there. This trip will be good for you and your mom, plus it means a lot to her, she had said, trying to convince me. As much as I had refused, my dad insisted that I come. *When will my life be mine to live?* I had asked myself that a million times over the last year. Everyone was making decisions that were best for them, forgetting what I might want or what might be best for me.

As we turned onto the lane, I could hear the sound of the gravel crunching under the weight of the tires. We drove slowly around the circular drive and stopped in front of the big white farmhouse.

"We're here," Aunt Abby said.

"Great…what a fun-filled week this will be." My sarcasm filled the air. I unbuckled my seat belt and reluctantly opened the car door.

"Just give it, and your mom, a chance," I heard her say as I stepped out of the car.

I stood, looking at the house in front of me. It seemed so much smaller than I remembered. I had always looked forward to visiting the ranch. We had come every year since my mom and Tom have gotten married, but this time, it was different. I was different.

Everything else still looked the same. The brick steps that led up to the porch that wrapped all the way around to the back of the house. A big wide farmhouse door with large panes of leaded glass. A screen door that snapped shut, just like the one at Aunt Abby's beach house. The big porch swing at one end was still there, just as I remembered. I recalled sitting in it at night with Poppie, listening intently to his stories. Stories of Indians that would turn into wolves and how they watched over the land that his family had owned for years. That I would never have to be afraid of anything…they would protect me.

A feeling of sadness began to come over me as I thought of Poppie, that he might not even be able to sit in the swing with me as he had every other time I had been here. He had been like a granddad to me, especially since I never knew mine.

My dad's parents had both died before I was born. My mom's parents had divorced long ago, and they too had passed away when I was little. She didn't talk about them much, and when she did mention them, it just seemed to make her sad, and she was quick to change the subject. *We'll talk about it someday*, she always said. But someday had not come yet.

Aunt Abby walked around the front of the car and stood beside me. "It is so beautiful here," she said.

We looked out at the grassy meadows that seemed to reach all the way to the mountain. I could smell the freshness in the air as the breeze blew across the sea of green grass, a clean, spring-like smell, with a hint of lavender, the grass swaying in the breeze. The mountain range was, in a weird way, as majestic as the ocean. *Almost*, I thought as I heard the snap of the screen door.

"You're here." It was my mom. She ran down the steps and hugged both of us at the same time. "I'm so glad you decided to come, honey, and, Abby, it is so good to see you. How was your flight?" She kissed my cheek, taking my hand in hers.

"Good," Aunt Abby said. At the same time, I sighed a response of "too long."

"Isn't it just beautiful here?" my mom said, squeezing my hand. "You can see why Tom doesn't want to let go of this place. He loves it here, and we'll love it too." She glanced out toward the mountain range.

"You can love it all you want." I pulled my hand from her grasp. "I'm only here for two weeks."

"I'm sure you already do, Joni. And we will do our best to make it as enjoyable and memorable as we can for all of us, while we're here. Won't we, Luvy?" Aunt Abby always had a way to calm me down.

"Sure," I said under my breath but managed a smile.

She took Aunt Abby by the hand and began leading her up the steps to the porch. "We'll get your things a little later. Let's go inside and relax for a little while first. Coming, honey?" She smiled, looking back at me.

"Coming…but just so you know, it wasn't me who decided to come." As soon as I said it, I felt bad, and a part of me wondered why I said the things I did. I could see the hurt it caused on her face.

I headed up the steps and followed them into the house. As the door closed behind me, I looked around the familiar room. A room filled with an odd combination of Poppie's things and pieces of furniture from our house… what used to be our house in Ohio.

I walked around the living room, touching things, as if by touching them, they would bring back a feeling that I had been longing for. A sense of home that I had not felt since my mom and Tom had packed up and moved here, and I had gone to stay with my dad. I understood that this was Tom's family home, but what about our family? Our house, our lives…is that not just as important?

Obviously not, I thought to myself as I could hear my mom and Aunt Abby talking in the kitchen.

"Tom had a meeting this afternoon with some of the other ranch owners. Something is going on with some of the cattle. He'll be home in time for dinner though. Are you guys hungry? I can fix us some lunch."

"Here, let me help." I watched as Aunt Abby opened the refrigerator and took out a pitcher of tea, setting it on the counter. She began opening the tall cabinet doors until she found the one containing the glasses she would use for lunch. Their voices trailed off as I wandered from the room into the screened-in porch that was attached just off the living room. The room felt cool…shaded by the big oak trees that hovered over the back yard. Trees that I had climbed so many times on my summer visits here. I had also been convinced that at night, these same trees would become monsters. Poppie would try to reassure me that they were guardians that protected the house and his loved ones. Now they didn't seem so big and scary, and as I looked at their intertwined limbs and branches, I realized how beautiful they were.

The leaves rustled gently in the breeze, feeling cool against my skin as it blew through the screens of the windows that lined that side of the porch. My eyes shifted to the opposite end of the room; I could see a big leather chair facing the windows where you could look out at the mountains. I had never thought too much about the beauty of them until now. It was like I was seeing them for the first time.

"It is so beautiful here." I used the same expression Aunt Abby had just a few moments earlier.

"Huh?" The grunt came from the direction of the big high-back chair. As I walked over and looked around the chair, I could see that Poppie was sitting there. He was just looking out the window. His expression never changed as I moved around the chair and knelt in front of him. My thoughts went back to Mr. Carlton as I recalled seeing him sitting in his chair, staring out at the water, and of all the events that had occurred that week. Events that had caused Mr. Carlton to make a choice that would cost him his life.

"Poppie." I placed my hand on his knee. His body jumped as if he had been shocked somehow. "I'm sorry, I didn't mean to scare you." His expression did not change as he turned to look down at me. I leaned up and kissed his cheek. Again, he jumped as if he had been startled.

"It's okay," I tried to assure him. "I've been looking forward to coming to visit you, to sit in the swing in the evenings just like we always do, and hear you tell all my favorite stories." I lied about "the looking forward to part," but his stories were some of the best memories I had of my visits here.

Tears filled his eyes as he tried to speak. "I…," he muttered. A tear spilled out and ran down his face. I stood to my feet, leaned in, and again kissed him on the cheek.

"Don't worry," I said, "we will have our time. Like we have always done…just like you've always told me, except, this time…I will tell you the stories."

For the first time in a long time, I smiled a genuine smile. It felt good. "I'll be back." I turned and walked back into the kitchen where Mom and Aunt Abby were busily making lunch.

I watched them as they worked together. My mom gathering sandwich stuff from the refrigerator, and Aunt Abby putting ice in the glasses and beginning to pour the tea. *How alike they are and yet so different,* I thought as I sat down on one of the stools at the large island bar in the middle of this farmhouse kitchen.

"I'm not hungry." I picked up a glass of iced tea and began to take a drink. "Does Poppie just sit there all day? Are you guys doing anything to help him get better?"

"Luvy!" The tone in her voice let me know that Aunt Abby was not happy with my questions.

"I need to get something out of the car." I set down my glass and stood to walk out of the kitchen.

"Christi, honey, we are all trying to do the best we can. That includes Poppie," my mom said.

"She'll be all right, she just needs a little more time." I heard Aunt Abby as I let the big door close behind me.

I took the bag that I had used as my carry-on for the flight from the back seat of the car, carried it up the steps onto the porch, and sat down on the big porch swing. It contained my phone, my tablet, a book I had intended to read on the flight, gum, and some other stuff. But most importantly, there was the box...his box. I set the bag down beside me and began to push the swing. Back and forth, back and forth.

I closed my eyes as my thoughts drifted back to the day I had left Ben on the dunes. I could almost feel his touch. I felt his lips touch mine. So much had happened that week, so much I still did not understand. Only Ben could explain it.

"Ben, where are you?" I looked down as I brushed my fingers across the top of the box. I stopped the swing, picked up my bag, and walked back inside the house. I just wanted to get these two weeks over with.

"Am I sleeping in the same room, or has that changed too?" I started up the stairs that led to the bedrooms that filled the upper floor of the farmhouse.

"Yes, honey, I'll bring you a sandwich up in a little bit."

I didn't respond as I continued up the staircase and walked to the end of the long hall to the bedroom I had slept in each time we had come here, closing the big wooden door behind me.

Looking around the room, it was nothing like I remembered. It had been a room filled with old furniture that I always thought needed to be replaced. *Old people stuff.* Now, instead, it was filled with my things, from our home in Ohio. What had once been our home—my furniture... my bed...my things!

Everything was out on my dresser just as it always had been. I walked over and picked up a frame that had a picture of me with my mom and my dad when I was about five years old. It was my favorite of the few photos I had of the three of us together. I set it down and walked over and sat on the side of the bed. Fresh-cut flowers were in a vase on the table beside the bed. I reached out and pulled a daisy from the bouquet.

He loves me...he loves me not, I thought as I pulled the petals off one by one. *He loves me.* I smiled as I looked at the single remaining delicate petal. Setting the bag that I had carried up on the bed beside me, I slowly slid the zipper of one of the compartments to the side and took out the folded piece of paper.

PRINCESS, he had written on the outside. I unfolded the letter and reread it for the hundredth time. Words on one of the only pieces of evidence I had that Ben even existed. That, and the box he had given to me that day. The box that contained pictures and memories of his family. They each gave me hope that he would find me.

They also served as reminders that the events of that week had not been a dream. That he was real and what I had seen in the water...what I had heard in the water...

was real. I had not told anyone about it. Everything had gone back to normal after we left the beach that day. Their normal.

No one talked about it, not even Aunt Abby. I think they thought I didn't want to talk about it. But the fact was, I did want to talk about Ben. I wanted to know about my time in the hospital...of the things I couldn't remember... what he said when he was there with me.

But some things had happened I knew I couldn't talk about. At least not until I spoke to Ben. I had to know he was safe. Until then, I could not chance to talk about it. Not that anyone would listen to me anyway. Who would believe that aliens had come to this world in search of survival...only to have saved it from destruction and that Ben had been the biggest part of it? That what happened to me in the water that night had changed me...in ways that I don't even fully know or understand. I had been very careful not to let anyone see what I knew was happening to me.

I looked at the word written on the front of the letter again, remembering how I had hated it when he called me that...now, I longed to hear it. *I would do anything to hear him call me that again,* I thought as I turned the paper over.

I know how much you hate it when I call you that. Do you believe in fate? I do. That we all have a destiny, and no matter how hard we may try to change it, some things are just how they are meant to be. Even though we may not be able to stop things from happening, we can affect the results. And that's why we are all here...to see what we do with what's given to us. I am better for having met you. Don't forget me. I hope you find your Prince Charming...isn't that the destiny of a princess?

Fate...destiny...don't forget me. Those were not just meaningless words on a piece of paper.

I will find you. I remembered his words.

"I know you will." I refolded the simple white paper and gently touched it to my lips.

Chapter Two

"Lunch is ready!" My mom opened the door to the bedroom.

"Just set it on the dresser." I folded the letter and tucked it into the back pocket of my jeans.

She walked over and placed the tray of food on the wooden piece of furniture. "Honey, I know how hard this move has been on you." She turned and sat down beside me. "You know how much Tom and I love you. We want you to be here with us. I'm not going to ask you to give up your senior year of high school and move out here, though. You can make the decisions that you feel are best for you. It's okay." She reached over and tucked my hair behind my ear. "I just want you to enjoy your time here, even if it's just for a couple of weeks. Okay?"

"Okay." I laid my head on her chest; tears began to roll down my face. "Why does everything have to change?"

"Oh, honey, nothing stays the same for long, and sometimes, that's what makes life exciting. We have so much to catch up on. You know, your dad's worried about you. He told me that you've quit the swim team? I know you've needed to regain some of your strength, honey, but you have to try to put what happened last year behind you." She wiped my tears and took my hand in hers. "You love swimming so much. I hate to see you just give it up." Looking down at my wrist, she rubbed her finger along the word *Princess* that was spelled out on the thin gold bracelet.

"You just said yourself that nothing stays the same, so maybe I am just tired of swimming, and it has nothing to do with what happened." I lied, knowing my love for swimming and the water would never change. "I've been running. I'm going to try out for track…maybe a change is good. It's not like I'm not doing anything. I'm fine," I lied again.

I got up from the bed and walked over to the window that faced the west side of the ranch. It was covered by a sheer white panel that filtered the brightness of the sun that was now shining above the mountain range. I was surprised at how much closer they seemed to be. Not nearly as far away as I remembered them to be.

She stood and walked over to stand beside me. "Will you do something for me?" she asked. I didn't respond as I looked out at the snow-capped peaks of the mountain range as the sun's rays reflected off them. "Will you promise to keep an open mind while you're here? We can take a look at the school."

"Mom!" I shouted at her. "Have you forgotten what you just said?" Making a statement more than asking a question.

"Okay…let's just see how it goes, and I promise I won't pressure you." She kissed the back of my head and turned to walk out of the bedroom just as we heard the sound of a car door closing.

I looked through the sheers to see that Tom's car had pulled in and had come to a stop on the circular drive. He got out and began to walk around the front of the vehicle toward the steps.

"It's Tom," I said as he disappeared from sight.

"Great, he's home early. We'll bring the rest of your things up so you can get settled in. I love you, honey." She looked back at me before she closed the door behind her.

"I love you too, Mom." I pulled the sheer curtain aside again and looked out past the driveway to the fields of nothingness that was this place my mom now called home.

I thought of Ben's words as I pulled the letter from my pocket. I held on to the single piece of paper where…somehow, within the words written there…contained a part of my heart. I let the curtain fall back into place, walked over, and took the box out of my bag, and set it on the stand by the bed. I opened the lid and placed the letter inside. Gently running my finger across the top. "But how could you ever find me here?"

I ate the chips from the plate she had brought, a couple of bites of the ham sandwich, all the while thinking about the conversations that I knew were coming when I went back downstairs. *A bath would postpone the inevitable and would help me feel better,* I decided. Being in water somehow always made me feel better.

Towels had been laid out in the bathroom that Aunt Abby and I would share. I turned on the hot water and began to undress. Standing in front of the mirror that hung on the back of the wooden door of the bathroom, nothing about the image that was staring back at me in the mirror seemed different. I thought about how normal I looked. But I knew—just as it had every time I had gotten into the tub since the day I had arrived home from the hospital—it would not be normal. I would not be normal as soon as the water covered my body. I didn't know what was happening. Just that it was…happening.

I stepped into the comfort of the water, and its warmth began to cover my body. I closed my eyes. Maybe if I kept them closed long enough, I wouldn't think about what I knew was happening to my body. That when I opened them, my body would be normal. That my eyes would be able to focus on my fingers and on my body all the way down to my toes.

But just as each time before, I opened my eyes, stretched out my hands under the water that had filled the tub, and looked at my fingers as they began to blur. I laid my head back against the hard iron rim of the tub, letting the water and its warm moisture saturate my skin. It felt good and familiar.

Concentrate, I told myself. *You can control it.* I knew what was happening, I just didn't know why. I needed Ben to answer that. I let the water flow over me as I soaked in the tub. I closed my eyes and slid under the water. How will I ever be able to compete again? *You have to be able to control this.* I don't know how much time passed when I opened my eyes and pulled myself from under the water. I released the lever to the drain and sat there as the water flowed from the tub. I stepped out of the bathtub and stood there as the water dripped from my body.

The reflection in the mirror was me but somehow… not me. It had been happening since I had gotten home from the hospital. In the beginning, I thought it was my eyes, and not my body, that was changing. But over the past months, I've come to realize, something had happened in the water that night. The night I had followed Ben and Mr. Carlton into the ocean. Something that had changed me, or at least a part of me. Water was causing my body to change somehow, in the same way Ben's body had changed that night. Into a vapor-like yet human-like form.

I just need to concentrate…harder, I thought. "You are normal, you are normal," I whispered out loud as I opened my eyes and stood there looking at the image in the mirror. An image that was now…completely normal. *And that's why I will not be on the swim team*, I reminded myself, as tears again began to well up in my eyes.

Get a grip, Christi, or you will never pull this off, I thought as I wrapped a towel around me and walked back to the bedroom. I could hear the muffled sounds of my family's voices coming from downstairs. Aunt Abby's laughter mixed with Tom's big booming voice. Although I couldn't make out what was being said, I had heard enough of Tom's stories that I could imagine his telling of a fantastic tale that he would exaggerate to make it more exciting and, of course, funnier. That was the one thing I loved most about Tom, he liked to laugh and to make us laugh.

My bag was sitting on the bed. It had been brought up while I was in the tub. I began to unpack and put my things away in the dresser that I had had since I was ten years old.

It seemed so out of place in this room. Everything seemed out of place.

"Luvy," I heard Aunt Abby as she knocked lightly on the bedroom door. She opened the door and stepped inside. "I just wanted to check on you, make sure you are okay." She walked over and took my hands in hers. She stood there looking at me waiting for me to respond.

"This was supposed to be our time. Our time at the beach. Why did we have to change our plans just because she chose to move here? Why couldn't we have just gone to South Carolina, just the two of us, like we always have?"

"Luvy, we talked about this."

I pulled my hands away and walked over to the window and stood with my back to her.

"This is hard for your mom too," she continued softly. "I think we should try to support her in this transition. We can still go to the beach after school starts, in the fall on break if we want." She paused for a moment. "This is not all about the beach, is it? I think that this may be more about Ben." I could feel my body tense, but I didn't turn to look at her. "I talked to Nancy Carlton a few weeks ago, she has not heard from him either. I'm sure he's fine, Luvy. He knows who to contact if he wanted to get in contact with you. When he's able to contact you, I mean." She corrected herself as if she knew I didn't want to think that he might not want to get in contact with me.

"How is Mrs. Carlton doing?" I asked. "I think about her a lot, I'm trying to remember more about what happened that night."

"She's doing all right. It's been a big adjustment for her. I can't even imagine it." She paused for a moment. "She's thinking of selling their house at the beach. Bob always loved it more than she did, and she just doesn't want to keep both places now that he's gone."

"You won't ever sell our beach house, will you?" My heart began to pound. "Promise me you won't ever get rid of our house!" I turned to look at her, tears spilling out over my cheeks.

"No, I would never sell our home at the beach." She walked over to the window and put her arms around me. "Just as you said, that is our place. But we're together now. The one thing we do is to make wherever we are, and whatever we are doing…fun. So, why don't you get dressed." She looked at me as I was still wrapped in a bath towel. "Come down and let's start planning our first week before your mom begins taking over." She smiled, gave me that wink, and turned to walk out of the room.

"I love you, Aunt Abby."

She stepped into the hallway. "To the moon and back," she responded as the door closed.

I pulled a bra and panties, a pair of shorts, and a T-shirt from the bag I had not yet finished unpacking. As I dressed, I thought about the conversation that I knew was coming when I went downstairs. Even though she said she was not going to pressure me, I knew my mom…pressure was what she was best at. The school here was starting in a few weeks. My senior year, I should be excited about planning for college, a swimming scholarship. But instead, all I could think of was what had happened. I knew what I knew, but what was killing me was what I didn't know. Not knowing where Ben was, what he was doing, and what he meant when he said he wasn't the only one who had stayed behind. If that was a good thing? If he was even okay? I guess in reality, I did know what he meant. Just not who or how many? Where they might be and what the future would hold.

Mostly my thoughts were of Ben. I walked over to the window and again pulled the curtains to the side of the freshly cleaned glass. Another thing my mom was good at…cleaning.

I looked out over the meadow that spread beyond the side yard to the big barn where the horses were kept. I had loved riding on our visits here. Poppie had taught me, and just like swimming, it had come naturally to me.

I started to turn away when something caught my eye. It was a pick-up truck heading up the dirt lane leading in from the field toward the barn. It stopped short of the barn. A man got out of the driver's side, the passenger door opened, and a girl got out. She had long brown hair and looked to be about my age. She had a noticeable limp as she walked toward the door of the barn where the man was waiting for her. *Must be her dad,* I thought, as he slid it open. I wondered who they could be as she followed him into the barn. I stood there watching, wondering why my mom had not mentioned that they had someone working on the ranch.

Just then the girl came back out of the barn. She was leading one of the horses. It was Midnight, the one I had always ridden. She turned and led him through the gate at the side of the barn. Closing it behind her, she mounted him. She leaned down and rubbed his face and mane, pulled on the reins, and rode off into the field.

*Hum…*maybe *we would have something to talk about, after all,* I thought as I turned away from the window, grabbed my phone, and walked out of the bedroom, closing the door behind me.

"Hey, Luvy," Aunt Abby said as I walked into the kitchen.

"There's my girl," Tom said. He came around the table where they were all sitting and reached to give me a big bear hug like he always did.

"Hey, Tom." I hugged him back.

"Are you all unpacked and settled in?" he continued, grabbing my hand, leading me as we went back to the table. Aunt Abby patted the chair beside her. I sat down beside her on the big wooden chair.

I turned to Tom, ignoring his question. "Who are the people that are tending to the horses? I saw a man and some girl go into the barn, she came back out and rode off on Midnight. Are they looking after the horses? Who are they?" I asked again before he could respond.

"Yes, that would be Manny and his daughter, Anna. They not only take care of the horses, but they help out here at the ranch too. She's your age, you know. She loves the horses, and this will be her first full year at school here too, so you two will have some things in common."

"Me? I'm not going to school here," I protested.

"Tom," my mom interrupted, "we've decided we are not going to talk about that right now."

"We, as in you and me," I gestured to her, "are not going to decide anything at all. I have already decided." I sat there, staring down at the table. Everyone was quiet.

"That's okay, then maybe you can get to know Anna while you are here," Tom continued, trying to change the subject. "She is a great young lady, hasn't met too many other kids her age yet, so she could use a friend."

"Maybe it will be good for both of you," my mom chimed in.

I was just about to let them know that they had no clue what would be good for me when Aunt Abby took my hand in hers. Sometimes just her touch had a way of calming me down.

"How long have they been helping out?" she asked.

"Just since spring," Tom answered. "We couldn't do it without them, that's for sure."

"What happened to her?" I asked. "Is there something wrong with her leg?"

"They were in a bad car accident when she was little, a drunk driver hit them. The accident killed her mom. She's had to have lots of surgeries on her leg, and lucky she didn't lose it...or worse," Tom explained as he poured himself a glass of tea.

"Oh no," Aunt Abby sighed. "That must have been awful for them, how old was she?"

"Around ten, I think, and yes, she has had a difficult time adjusting. I've had a few conversations with Manny about it. I know that she's had trouble making friends, keeps to herself a lot. She loves working with the horses though," Tom said, looking at me. "Maybe you two can ride together?"

Aunt Abby tightened her hand around mine. "That sounds like a great idea, doesn't it, Luvy?"

"Yes, actually it does." I managed a smile as I squeezed her hand.

Chapter Three

"I told Pop I would take him out with me this evening."
Tom walked over to my mom and kissed her on the cheek.
"We are going to make a run up to the north fence line,
just to make sure it does not need some repairs. We've got
to figure out how whatever it is that's killing the cattle is
getting in."

"You don't know what it is?" Aunt Abby asked.

"We're not sure. Could be animals. Maybe a pack of
wolves. But if it is, they're not hunting for food. They're
just out for the kill, leaving them there just to bleed out."

"What does that mean, what animal would do that?"
Aunt Abby frowned.

"I don't know, might not be an animal at all. Could
be kids...some ritual or something. Things are crazy
anymore."

"Oh, surely not!" Aunt Abby gasped, cupping her
hands to her face.

"We just need to find out before we lose the whole herd." He walked around the table and started into the living room.

"Don't you want to eat dinner first?" my mom asked.

"I need to check it out now. Keep it warm for us," he smiled. "Christi, do you want to ride along with us? I'm sure Pop would like that, I know I would."

"Sure, why not." I stood to follow him into the living room.

"You guys be careful, and try to be home before dark," my mom called out as we walked through the living room onto the porch where Poppie was still sitting.

"Pop, you ready to take that ride?" His expression never changed as Tom knelt beside him. "Except this time we're going to have company. Christi is going along with us. I'm going to bring the truck around, okay?" Tom patted his dad on the shoulder, nodded at me, and started out the side door of the porch.

"I remember you taking me with you when you went out to feed the cows." I leaned over as I spoke to Poppie. "It was one of the things I loved most about being here, spending time with you." He just sat there, staring straight ahead. "Don't you remember?" I softly put my hand on his shoulder, hoping for some sign that maybe he did. He began to fidget in his chair as if he were uncomfortable. "Are you okay, Poppie?" I asked, looking down at him.

Tom pulled the truck to the side entrance and came up onto the porch. "Ready?" he asked. "Christi, can you help us?" Together we raised him to his feet by lifting him under his arms.

"Oh!" he murmured, groaning as he slowly stood. We held on to his arms to help him steady himself, then we began to walk toward the screen door that led to the wrap-around driveway where the truck was parked.

"See, Pop, you are doing much better today."

"Yeah, you are doing great," I tried to encourage him. He shuffled his feet as we moved slowly across the wooden floor of the screened-in porch.

The passenger-side door was open. I slid in and tried to help as Tom lifted Poppie onto the seat. We turned him and raised his legs inside the truck. I helped as much as I could, but I could tell this had become a routine that they had gotten used to. It made me sad seeing this once strong man that I had known...now so helpless. But somehow, at the same time, a feeling of ease came over me. I tried to get him as comfortable as possible and pulled the seat belt across his lap.

"Good to go," Tom said reassuringly. The belt clicked into place. Poppie looked straight ahead. He had a look of contentment on his face; he knew exactly what was happening, and he was pleased.

We headed down the drive leading away from the house. "It's nice of you to do this for your dad." I knew my stepdad was a good man. One who loved his whole family...including me. I didn't blame him for the changes in our lives.

"We are just trying to keep things somewhat normal for him, for as long as we can," he replied.

"Normal! What's that?"

"You've had to adjust to a lot of changes too, and you went through quite an ordeal last spring, didn't you? Are you doing all right?"

"Yeah...I'm okay," I murmured. But what I really wanted to do was scream *No...I am not okay, everything has changed, I am not normal. Nothing is the same as it was before, nor will it ever be the same again. I need help, I need your help.* Instead, I just stared blankly out the window as we drove down the dirt lane toward the gate that led out into the pasture.

We pulled in front of the gate and stopped. "You know your mom and I are here for you if you ever need to talk." I just nodded my head and looked away so he wouldn't see the tears welling up in my eyes. "She only wants the best for you, you know. She also wants to spend as much time with you as she can. We never know how much time we have, nothing in this life is guaranteed."

"Then she should not have moved out here!" I wiped away a tear that had begun to roll down my cheek. "She could have stayed in Ohio...with me."

"Christi, it's not that simple. Your mom didn't want me to have to make a choice between taking care of my dad and the ranch and doing what was fair for us as a family." He was trying to justify her decision.

"And so she chose you! She had a choice between you and me...she chose you!" I could feel the hurt and anger building inside me.

"I'm sure she was hoping you wouldn't think of it as choosing one over the other. She always felt that you would understand the decision we made and would support it, even if you didn't agree with it." He was looking at me. "I'll get the gate."

We pulled to a stop at the outer fence. Tom got out and slid the big metal gate to the side.

I didn't say anymore as we headed to the north pasture where most of the cattle grazed. Just Tom's random attempts at small talk with an occasional comment to Poppie about the fencing and the surroundings. I stayed silent and expressionless as the truck creaked and bounced across the bumpy fields.

Tom stopped the truck suddenly. "Wow!" he gasped.

I stared out of the windshield into the field ahead of us. "Oh no!" was all I could manage to say. I felt the anger draining from my body; it was replaced with dread, that same sinking feeling I had felt before.

There, in the field ahead of us were dead cows. Lots of dead cows. Flies were swarming their bodies. It reminded me of the sea of dead fish that had washed ashore when we were in South Carolina. But we were not in South Carolina; we were in Wyoming, and these were cows, not fish.

We just sat there for what seemed like forever. "Aren't you going to get out?" I finally broke the silence.

"No, there is nothing we can do right now. Plus, we need to be careful. We have no idea what this might be, it could be a disease or something. Let's get back so I can make some phone calls." He began to turn the truck around.

"What do you think is happening?" I looked across the bed of the truck as we headed back across the field.

"I don't know what it is, but I know what it is not. I could use some of your wisdom about now, Pop."

He leaned forward and looked across the truck at Poppie who had not moved and was still staring straight ahead.

"It's not wolves." Both of us looked at him as he spoke plainly and matter-of-factly. Suddenly, we hit a rut in the field that rattled and shook the whole truck.

We traced our way back across the dirt lane that led back to the farmhouse. I could see the man Tom had called Manny sitting on the steps in front of the house as we pulled around the circular drive. Tom motioned to him as we drove around the side to the door of the porch.

I was just about to get out when the passenger-side door opened. "Hey, little lady," Manny said, smiling. His cheerfulness upset me somehow. He began to help Poppie with his seat belt.

"My name is Christi," I snapped, sliding across the green vinyl seat and out of the driver's side door.

"I know. We have heard so much about you. Anna's been excited to meet you."

I ignored him, closing the door of the truck.

"Manny and I will get Pop inside. Why don't you go, let your mom know we're back?" Tom said as they began to slowly make their way to the back porch.

"Sure." I walked back toward the front of the house. "Mom, Aunt Abby, we're back." I let the screen door close behind me.

"Great! That was quick," Mom said. They were still in the kitchen, at the table, in the same places they were when we left.

"The cows are all dead."

"Oh no!" they said at the same time, turning to look at me.

"Tom and that guy are bringing Poppie in around back."

"It's bad," Tom said as they entered the kitchen. "I'm going to call Dr. Baker and see if he can meet us first thing in the morning before the whole town gets wind of what's happening. Don't want people jumping to their own conclusions."

"Any ideas about that. What's happening, I mean?" Aunt Abby asked.

"I've got some ideas, but I hope we can get some real answers soon." He looked worried.

"So it is not another animal, coyotes, or wolves?" my mom asked, shrugging her shoulders, shaking her head.

"Pop doesn't think so," he winked at me. "Truth is, we just don't know yet. Manny and I are heading up to the upper north pasture to check on the rest of the herd. We'll try to be back before dark." He kissed my mom on the cheek and turned to head out onto the porch.

"Nice to see you, Ms. Joni, Miss Christi, Ma'am." Manny nodded toward Aunt Abby and followed Tom through the front door.

"Be careful," Mom called to them.

"Sit tight, Pop," he yelled out as the screen door snapped shut.

The engine of the truck started, and the sound of the gravel cracking under the weight of it pulling out of the drive filled the room.

I walked over and opened the refrigerator, grabbed a bottle of water, and stood at the sink looking out at the barn.

Anna was leading Midnight around the pen. "What is she doing out there?"

"Who?" my mom asked. "Anna? Why don't you go introduce yourself and find out?"

Okay, I thought. "Can I take Midnight out?"

"Honey, it's getting late. It'll be dark soon. Why don't you wait until tomorrow," she said.

"See, when are you ever going to let me grow up and make my own decisions?" I snapped at her. "I told you, Aunt Abby, these two weeks will be all about her."

"Then promise me you will not ride too far, not until we know for sure what is going on. And only if you'll stay in the pasture behind the barn." I was surprised that she had changed her mind so quickly and was actually going to let me take him out.

"Are you sure you are not too tired?" Aunt Abby asked. "Like your mom said, you can always take him out tomorrow." She was covering for her...again. "We do have two weeks."

"Won't go by soon enough." I gave her that *look* as I walked out of the kitchen and through the front door.

"Take your phone," I heard my mom say. I felt my pocket to make sure it was there and headed down the steps before she had a chance to change her mind.

Anna was brushing down Midnight just outside the barn. "Hey." I walked up and leaned against the wooden fence that surrounded the barn.

38

"Hey back." She smiled as she looked over at me. "I was just about to put Midnight in the barn. I'll be right back." She started to lead the beautiful horse into the open barn doors.

"Don't bother. I'm taking Midnight out, so you can just tie him off at the gate. Hey, Midnight," I said as I watched her take him around the side of the barn and tie him onto one of the gate posts. A slight feeling of jealousy came over me. I wasn't sure that I liked the idea that someone else was doing some of the things that I had always helped Poppie with when I was here during the summer.

She walked back over to where I was standing, climbed up the rungs of the fence, and sat on the top rail.

"I've heard so much about you. I'm so glad that you're here. I've been here by myself—well, not technically by myself, there is my dad, but with no one my age to talk to for what seems like forever, I thought I was about to go crazy." She was rattling away so fast, I could hardly keep up. "I'm going to be a senior too…I hope we have some of the same classes, I'm sure we will." She never stopped for a breath, she just kept talking. "Can we go together to orientation this week? It's just a walkthrough, getting familiar with classrooms and all, schedules and meeting the teachers. If we go together, we will at least know someone. Maybe you know some people here, but I don't, not really anyway. I've been really nervous about going to a new school, but since you are here, it will be a lot better."

"Wait, slow down!" I finally interrupted her. "I am not going to school here. I am just here for a few days to visit. I don't know where you got that idea. Sorry, you are on your own with that one." I was already getting annoyed with her. "Besides, I thought you were already in school here?"

"But I thought Ms. Snyder, I mean your mom, said you would be coming to stay and start school here this fall? I only went for a few weeks at the end of the last school year, I didn't get to know anyone really. Except for Liam. The girls are not very nice here."

"Ok, first off, let's get one thing straight. My mom, Ms. Snyder, says a lot of things, but she doesn't make decisions for me. I am just here with my aunt for a couple of weeks." I stared in the direction in which Tom and her dad headed just a few minutes earlier.

"Don't you want to be here with your mom?"

"I thought you were supposed to be really quiet?" I gave her a look that was meant to let her know that she was a little too personal with her questions.

"I'm sorry." She looked in the direction the truck had gone. "I just wish I had another opportunity to be with my mom."

I turned to look up at the girl sitting beside me. She was small, maybe a couple inches shorter than me. Her beauty was reflective of her Mexican heritage, with long dark straight hair that flowed down her back, flawless tan skin, and big brown eyes. *No wonder the girls are mean to you,* I thought, *they're jealous.*

"I'm sorry about your mom, the accident and all, I mean." I felt awkward even bringing up the subject of her losing her mom.

She looked straight ahead. "I wish I could just have one more day with her. Don't get me wrong, I love my dad and all, he is my whole world now. But there are just some things that you need to talk to your mom about, you know what I mean. Like makeup, boys, things you just can't talk to your dad about. What to do, what to feel, when girls say mean things to you." She never looked at me as she spoke. "How could you not want to live with your mom? You should be with her every moment that you possibly can, you can never get that time back." She finally turned to look at me. Her sad brown eyes were filled with tears.

"You don't know me, how can you sit there and suggest what I should do," I shouted at her. Then instantly wishing I had kept my thoughts to myself.

"I'm sorry," she said. She reached out and touched my arm as if she was reading my thoughts. "It's really none of my business, and I'm not judging you."

"Well that's big of you." I pulled away and climbed through the wooden fence. "No wonder people are mean to you. Maybe you should practice keeping your opinions to yourself." I walked toward the barn, leaving her sitting on the fence.

I took the saddle and harness from Midnight's stall. She was still sitting on the top rail of the fence as I walked around the side of the barn and threw the saddle on his back.

"Hey, handsome." I rubbed Midnight's mane and kissed the side of his head. "Want to go for a ride?" He shook his head as if to say *Yes!* I tightened the straps, untied his reins from the post, and swung open the gate.

I could hear them coming as I began to lead him through. It was Anna leading Summer, another beautiful horse that Poppie has had for years.

"Okay if we go with you?"

"It's a big pasture." I looked back at her. "Sure." My tone softened as I pulled myself up into the saddle.

She closed the gate and effortlessly swung herself up onto Summer. "I know the perfect place," she said, riding ahead of me.

"Wait, my mom said to stay close to the barn," I called out to her as I nudged Midnight's sides to catch up.

"I thought you said your mom doesn't make your decisions for you?" She stopped and looked back at me. I stopped beside her. We just sat there looking at each other, waiting for me to respond.

"Then prove it." She jerked on Summer's reins and rode off across the field toward the base of the mountain.

When I caught up with her, we rode side by side until we reached the outer fence line. She dismounted long enough to open the wooden gate that kept the horses safely near the barn. She handed me the reins of her horse and closed the gate behind us.

Chapter Four

We stayed silent as I again fell in stride behind her, letting her lead the way. It was evident that she knew where she was headed. I had never ridden out this far before. Poppie had never let me go past the outer gate. I knew we should not be doing it now, but it didn't stop me. It seemed I had become accustomed to going against the rules.

We began to wind our way around the base of the mountain range. Looking back toward the ranch house that was now out of view, I realized how small and insignificant everything seemed. I felt an overwhelming sense that there was something so much bigger than we could ever imagine happening all around us.

"Do you even know where you are going, or are you just riding?" I yelled up at her.

"You'll see" was all she said.

I looked up at how beautiful and grand the mountains were as they towered over the green grasslands beneath them. It was early July, and there were still snow caps on the peaks. The ice and snow would not dissolve till late summer, and some areas would never completely melt. I stopped just long enough to take a couple of pictures with my phone. We made our way along the narrow trail that was cut into the mountainside, both by man and animals coming down the mountain looking for food and water. I thought of the dead cows. If they had been killed by animals, why would they have killed them if they had not been looking for food? And if it was not animals, then what was it? A chill ran through me.

"How much further?" I tried not to sound concerned, knowing my mom would freak out the longer we were gone.

We rounded a bend in the path. "Almost there," she answered.

I could hear it before I saw it. There ahead of us, cascading over the mountainside, over the rocks and into a big pool of water at its base, was the most beautiful waterfall I had ever seen. It was like something you would see in a movie or a magazine. It flowed out into a small creek that snaked around the base of the mountainside.

"Wow, I see why you come out here, this is gorgeous. I didn't even know this was here. Is this even still on Poppie's property?" I asked, in awe of the beauty that surrounded us.

"No," she answered.

"Whose property is it?"

"It belongs to the Bakers...Liam Baker's family. It's okay, though. They won't care. Liam's actually the only nice person our age that I've met since we've been here." She smiled back at me, slid off Summer, and slowly led her to the stream. She dropped the reins as the horse began to drink from the water that was rippling through the creek. I did the same as Midnight too began lapping at the crystal-clear water. "I think it's a hidden treasure. It's where I come when I need to get away. I feel close to my mom here somehow," she said softly as she sat down on the grassy bank beside the water.

"I have a place just like that. A place where I feel like I'm close to someone when I'm there." I thought of the dunes at our beach house in South Carolina. The unique connection Ben and I had shared there.

"A boy?" She stood and took a few steps toward the waterfall.

"You really should learn to mind your own business." I made my way alongside the pool of water, looking at the reflection of the mountain in the glass-like surface of the water.

"Come on," she waved to me. "You can walk under the waterfall and not even get wet." She walked toward the rocks that surrounded the base of the waterfall. I followed her as she carefully made her way from stone to stone, stepping on the rock ledge that lined the wall of rock behind the waterfall. "Stay close to the wall," she warned.

Don't worry, I thought. I could not take the chance to get too close to the stream of water. "This is so cool," I said. We made our way across the ledge, feeling the cool mist from the wall water that was flowing in front of us.

"Look…see the rainbow?" She pointed into the mist. We looked through the beautiful colors as the sun's rays reflected on the flowing water.

"Amazing!" I whispered, taking my phone out of my pocket to capture its beauty. "Here, let's get a selfie." We smiled, squeezing our faces together to capture the waterfall and the rainbow's effect behind us.

We walked back across the ledge, again carefully maneuvering our way over the glistening rocks to the other side of the pool.

"What are you doing?" I asked as she kicked off her shoes. "That water comes from the top of the mountain, you will freeze your feet off." I glanced over the waterfall to the mountain peaks. "You are not going to get in, are you? Seriously, that water has to be freezing." I looked at her in disbelief.

She began to unzip her jean shorts, slid them down her legs, and stepped out of them. She pulled her top over her head and stood there in her underwear.

"I've been waiting to do this since I've been coming here," she squealed as she jumped into the pool of water. "Oh my gosh! You were right, it's cold," her voice broke as she swam out into the middle of the water.

"Dude! Are you crazy?" I looked at her knowing that, *yes*, she really must be crazy.

"I'm kidding. It's not cold at all. Come on in." She motioned to me with a wave of her hand.

"No way! No freaking way! Ocean water, chlorinated pool water, hot tubs I can do…I'm not getting into a giant, freezing ice bucket of water." What I was saying was true, but in the back of my mind, I knew what would happen to my body if I got into the water. The same thing that had been happening for months now. No, I would not be swimming with her today or any other day.

"You are crazy," I laughed as she splashed and played in the water like a little kid. "Anna, it's getting late, I think we need to start back, it's going to start to get dark soon." I stood and walked a little closer to where she was treading in the water.

"Oh, come on, seriously, it's not cold, believe it or not, it's kind of warm, and besides, it won't be dark for a couple of hours." She tried to plead her case.

"Yeah, right, I've heard that before. Besides, see." I pointed to the shadow that the mountain was beginning to cast on the water close to the waterfall.

"Come on, it's the one place I feel normal, where I don't worry about my leg." She began to swim toward the falls.

It was then that something caught my eye. A flash of light under the water near the base of the waterfall. A flash of light that was all too familiar to me. One that I saw every night in my dreams.

"Get out," I screamed. "Anna, get out now!"

"Calm down, why are you so anxious? Come on, get in, it's not that cold." She splashed water in my direction. The warm water splashed against the side of my face as I stood frozen in place.

I had not taken my eyes off the round circular ball of light that was still there, just below the surface of the water, near the waterfall.

Maybe it is just a reflection from the sun off one of the shiny rocks, I told myself. *Like the ones that were all around the base of the falls.*

"Anna, get your ass out of the water."

"What is it?" she asked. "Is it a snake?" She looked around, glancing toward the waterfall.

The sphere of light was still there. It was exactly like the ones that were engrained in my memory ever since the night I had followed Ben and Mr. Carlton into the water.

"Please, Anna, I'm serious, get out of the water," I pleaded again.

She was looking at me now as if I were the crazy one. "Okay…okay." She made her way to the side of the pool of water and lifted herself onto the grassy bank.

I glanced at her, then back to the spot where the light had been. It was gone. Nothing, just crystal-clear blue water. I suddenly felt a little foolish. The thought that what I might have seen could somehow be the same as what was in the water in South Carolina was ridiculous. Or was it? *Could it be Ben? No…Ben would have let me know he was here. Certainly not in this way. It couldn't possibly be one of the others he had talked about, could it?* I wondered to myself, as a shiver ran down my spine.

"Promise me you will not swim here." I glared at her as she walked past me and began to put her clothes back on.

"I don't see the big deal. Just like you, I'm a big girl. Besides, it really isn't that cold."

"Promise me!"

"All right, I'll play along. I'll promise you if you promise me something."

"This is not a game, Anna." She was really irritating me now.

"Go to the open house at school with me this week, and I will…promise, I mean."

There was a part of me that instantly wanted to push her back into the water. "You are seriously trying to make a deal with me right now!" I walked past her and grabbed Midnight's reins. I backed him away from the pool and pulled myself up into the saddle.

"Hey, wait for me," I heard her say. "I was just kidding, sort of. You don't have to go."

I had no intention of waiting. As soon as we cleared the narrow mountain trail, I ran Midnight the rest of the way to the barn. I knew she was back there, but I didn't turn around.

She entered the barn as I was putting Midnight into one of the stalls. "Why are you so mad at me?" she asked. "Why did you freak out? I can swim. I'm not a handicap just because of my leg. You don't have to be afraid I'll hurt myself." I walked past her toward the barn door. "You don't have to go to the open house." She was rattling again, as she followed me. "You said it yourself, you make your own decisions. Even though it would be nice to go to school with someone I know, I was only kidding. And I will go swimming in the waterfall if I want to, I don't understand what the big deal is."

She was right. She didn't understand, she couldn't. "I'm not mad at you." I stopped for a moment. I understood why she was confused by my reaction. "I'm sorry, I just overreacted. It's been a long day, and I am just tired." I walked out of the barn, across the yard and up the steps to the porch.

"It's okay!" I heard her yell. "I'm still glad you're here."

"Great, I wish I was," I mumbled.

The front porch light came on. My mom came out, closing the screen door behind her. "Anna, sweetie, do you want to come up and wait with us till your dad gets back?"

"No, thank you, Ms. Snyder, I need to finish with the horses."

I suddenly realized that I had just put Midnight in his stall without even brushing him down. "I'm sorry, Anna, I can come and help."

"No, it's okay. I got it. I'll see you tomorrow, though." She closed the door of the barn.

"You have to be tired, honey. Why don't you go up and shower and get ready for bed?" my mom said softly.

"Where is Aunt Abby?"

"She's already gone to bed, she was exhausted. It's been a long day for both of you."

"Are you going up, or are you going to stay out here?" I asked.

"No, I'm going to sit right here and wait for Tom to get back." She walked over to the porch swing. "You can sit with me if you want."

"You know, I am tired, so I think I'm going up for the night." I knew where that conversation would end up if I stayed out here with her.

"I promise we won't talk about anything you are not ready to," she smiled and patted the empty space on the swing beside her.

I walked over to the swing and sat down beside her as she put her arm around me. "Oh, honey, I have missed you so much," she kissed my forehead. I leaned over and laid my head on her lap.

"Scratch my back." She began to lightly run her fingernails down the length of my back, just like she had been doing ever since I could remember. "Under," I whispered. She gently pulled my T-shirt up just enough to scratch the skin underneath. "Don't stop…" I closed my eyes.

It was the crackling of the gravel that woke me. I raised up from Mom's lap, as Tom and Manny got out of the pickup.

"Thanks, Manny, we'll talk in the morning," I heard him say as he shook Anna's dad's hand and slapped him on the back.

"Both my girls still up." He smiled as he came up onto the porch.

"Not for long, I'm done." I leaned over, kissed my mom, and stood to give Tom a hug.

"Don't leave on my account." He walked over and sat down on the swing in the spot where I had been.

I turned to go inside. "I'm getting up early and going for my run," I said.

"I'm not sure that's a good idea," my mom said. "Not until we know for sure what's out there and what's going on."

"Great! I have track tryouts when I get home. So what, I'm just supposed to stay inside the whole time I'm here?" I barked at her.

"She'll be okay," Tom said calmly. "Just be careful, she knows to stay on the main road." He put his arm reassuringly around her.

"I guess I'm outnumbered," she sighed. "I'll be in and check on you when I come up."

"Did you get a chance to meet Anna?" Tom asked.

"Yeah, and just so you know…she is not quiet." I heard them laugh as I closed the screen door behind me.

I walked across the kitchen floor to the staircase that leads to the upper level. I heard a noise from the porch. "Poppie?" I walked over to the chair to find him sitting where he had been earlier. "You still awake?" I asked him. "Are you cold?" I picked up a blanket from the basket on the floor next to him and covered his legs with it. "Of course, you are still awake, we haven't had our story time yet, have we?"

I was talking to him; I knew he could hear me…yet his expression never changed. I took another blanket from the basket, wrapped it around me, and sat down on the floor beside him.

"Why don't I start?" I looked up at him. "What story can I tell you that you've not already heard? Or…maybe one that you have, only just in a slightly different way." I thought for a moment, then began.

"Not so long ago, but in a very, very faraway place, there was a people that came to our land in search of a new home. Looking for a life that could not only sustain them but would offer them a whole new way of existing. It was not a journey of choice or even something that they felt they had a choice in. It was their only way. So, only the bravest ventured out in hopes that they would find this new land. A land that offered life and freedom for their people. The journey was hard, so hard that only one managed to survive…or so he thought.

"Soon, he discovered others, too, had survived somehow. It would not be long before they found that there would be many obstacles they would have to face in this new land. They would be forced to find a way to survive. They did, but at the cost to those who had already settled in this land. Some wanted the land just for what it had to offer them, with little or no regard to how it might destroy it, their own selfish interests took over.

"But there was one. One that stood out from all of the others. One who would put the lives of others, and the needs of those who might come after him, ahead of his— forgetting what he wanted, needed…what he desired. And why did he do this we ask? Because he had fallen in love with the princess of the land. There was nothing he would not do for her. Even if it caused him to lose his life and the lives of his people, he would protect her.

"And so he did, but in doing so, he was never to see her again. That was the cost of her freedom and for all those that she loved. And every time she looks at the stars in the sky, she knows he is watching over her and protecting her still. Protecting her until the stars fall from the heavens." Tears streamed down my face as I finished the story. I stood and kissed him on the cheek.

"Good night, Poppie."

My bed had been turned down, and I wanted so badly to just crawl into it. Instead, I made my way across the hall to the bathroom. I slipped out of my clothes and turned on the shower. The tears were uncontrollable as I let the hot water run over my head and down my body. I braced my hands on the wall and leaned my head against the front panel of the shower. My tears mixed with the water as they ran down my face. They tasted like the saltwater of the ocean.

I thought of the story that I had shared with Poppie, and even though it was more reality than fiction, it felt good to talk about it. It felt good to let someone know what had happened...even in a story. "If it did even happen?" I said out loud. I slid down into the coolness of the tub and let the warm water shower over me.

My body was fading. It was there, but yet not there. A reminder that *Yes, Christi, it did happen.*

Chapter Five

I had come to dread going to sleep. Knowing my mind would not be able to relax. And although it had been hard for me to sleep, when I did, the dreams came. Just as they always did when I closed my eyes. The same as they had every night since Ben had pulled me out of the ocean in South Carolina. The night that everything began changing for me.

I was in the water, just like all the times before. Sinking, only tonight it was different. This time I was caught in a chamber of some kind. It was a glass cylinder. I could see all around me. Water was pouring in from the opening in the top, and no matter how hard I tried to swim to the surface, the pressure of the water pouring into the cylinder forced me back to the bottom. I told myself, *It's only a dream,* but the feeling was real...like my lungs were going to burst. *Wake up,* I told myself, but I couldn't seem to pull myself out of the world that was drowning me.

It was the buzzing sound from the alarm on my phone that saved me. I reached out to shut it off. *3:00 AM*, the screen read. *Thank you, Lord Jesus,* I thought as I threw the covers off. I sat on the side of the bed, wondering when or if the dreams would ever stop.

It seemed that I would always wake more tired than I was when I went to bed. I'd come to welcome the mornings, and the routines the light of day would bring. But this morning was going to be anything but routine. I was going back to the waterfall before the sun, or anyone else, got up.

I had seen something. *Could it be Ben?* I had to find out, without anyone knowing that I was going out in the middle of the night. So again, I was sneaking out, hoping I would be back before anyone discovered me being gone.

I slowly made my way to the bathroom. Flipping the light on, I caught a glimpse of myself in the mirror. *Ugh,* I looked like I hadn't slept in days. I turned the light back off. I brushed my teeth and quietly walked back to my bedroom, praying I would not wake Aunt Abby. Pulling clothes out of the dresser drawer, I managed to get dressed. Leggings, a T-shirt, and a sweatshirt—mornings here were always cold. I pulled my hair back into a ponytail, grabbed my Ohio State hat, and pulled the long strand of hair through the opening in the back. I slipped on a pair of socks and my favorite sneakers, unplugged my phone from the charger, and headed downstairs.

I tried to be as quiet as the creaky stairs would let me. I hugged the wall and crept down each rung, looking back up the stairway for any sign of movement. Everyone was still sleeping. I crossed the kitchen that was lit only by the dim light over the stove. The tight deadbolt lock clicked loudly as I turned it. I turned to see if there was any sign that someone might have heard it. Satisfied that everyone was still asleep, I opened it, stepped out onto the front porch, and closed it behind me, quietly letting the spring on the screen door pull it gently back into place.

I made my way to the barn and pulled open the drawer where I knew Tom had always kept a flashlight. The sun would not be up for a couple of hours, and in this valley surrounded by two mountain ranges, it always seemed like it took half the day before you could actually even see the sun.

I opened Midnight's stall. "Hey, handsome, ready for an early morning ride?" I kissed the side of his face, rubbing his neck and long thick mane. I took the saddle from the bench and began to prepare the beautiful horse for our journey, one that we had just made a few hours ago. I lead him out of the barn, then slid the huge barn door shut.

I turned and looked at the house. The light in Aunt Abby's bedroom came on. *Oh no,* I started to panic. I stood still, waiting for the curtain to pull back. I sighed in relief as the light in the bathroom flicked on.

"Let's go, boy," I whispered as I led Midnight around the side of the barn. I would just have to hope she would go back to bed without stopping by my room to check on me.

We made our way away from the barn and through the gate before I mounted Midnight. We headed out across the field. Stopping just long enough to open and close the outer gate, then we slowly made our way to the trail at the base of the mountain that led to the falls.

"I hope you can see much better than I can," I said to Midnight as I fought with the flashlight. I smacked it against my palm. It would shine for a moment and then dim. We climbed up the small bank onto the trail. The moon and stars were offering little help against the shadow of this magnificent mountain.

I continued to trace our tracks from yesterday, maneuvering very carefully until we reached a point where I had decided I should walk the rest of the way. I wanted to be as quiet as possible when I came upon the waterfall, not knowing for sure who or what I might find.

"You stay right here." I tied Midnight to a tree that was just off the trail. "I'll be back." I kissed him on his neck.

I carefully made my way along the narrow trail. I turned the flashlight on and off to help light up my way while trying to preserve what little battery it had left. I wasn't sure how long it would take me to get to the waterfall.

The sounds of the mountain filled the night air. Limbs cracking as the branches of the trees swayed against the wind that was blowing gently. The quiet scratching noises of the small ground animals that scurried to safety as I passed by. An occasional *who...who* of an owl. And somewhere, faintly in the distance, I thought I heard the howl of a wolf. I stopped and listened—nothing.

Too many Poppie stories, I thought as I continued toward the sound of the cascading water.

The flashlight dimmed suddenly and then went out. "Darn." I pounded it against the palm of my hand. It was no use, it was dead. "That's just great!" I shoved it into the pocket of my sweatshirt.

The moon seemed to be shining a little more brightly as I rounded the curve in the trail. I could hear the waterfall and faintly make out the white foam that was bubbling over the rocks and splashing into the pool below. It reminded me of the white caps that you could see at night along the beachfront in South Carolina.

I remembered how warm the water has been when Anna splashed it on me the evening before. Warm like the ocean. I thought about how much I had loved getting into the warm waters at the beach house. And how everything had changed since the last time I had been there.

As I neared the waterfall, I knelt down and peered into the dark pool of water that rippled from the force of the falls. It was dark and eerily quiet—no sign of any lights.

"Ben," I said out loud. Then thought about how stupid I sounded. As crazy as it would have looked and sounded to any sane person. But then a reasonable person would not believe Ben's story anyway, or any of what had happened. "Ben," I said again, hoping that by just wanting it to be, would make it so. That the light I had seen yesterday would suddenly appear and Ben would be here, standing in front of me.

I sat down on the edge of the water and put my face in my hands. I was caught somewhere between what seemed to be a fairy tale and a nightmare, and I did not know how to get out of it. Ben was the one link to the reality of it all. *I'm the crazy one,* I thought as I recalled the words I had spoken to Anna when we were here earlier.

"I may be crazy, but I have to know!" I took off my hat, clothes and shoes, leaving on only my panties and bra. I laid them along the bank and walked toward the water. I tried the flashlight one more time. Having no luck, I dropped it on the ground and slipped into the dark water. It suddenly made sense to me why the water had felt warm to Anna…if I had seen what I thought I had…*of course, it would be warm.* I swam toward the base of the falls, took a deep breath, and slipped quietly under the water.

I didn't move a muscle as I let my body sink under the water. Just an occasional movement of my hands to keep from rising to the surface. My body began to change.

Listening, I heard nothing. Just the muffled sound that the water made as it fell from the rock ledge above and plunged deep into the pool below. I forced my way deeper and deeper into the water. The surreal darkness surrounded me, but yet, it was peaceful. As peaceful as being in the water had always made me feel. I stopped to listen, still nothing but silence. *Ben,* I thought, knowing if he were here, he would somehow hear me. But also knowing that if it were one of the others, they too would hear me.

The shadows of the rocks beneath the falls loomed in the dark stillness under the water. The image was broken only by its churning, as it fell from above. My eyes began to adjust as a cave-like crevice came into focus. I swam toward the opening and through it without a thought of what I might encounter inside.

I wondered where it would lead or if it even led any-where. I knew it was not a good idea for me to be here if someone other than Ben were. *What would I do if someone were here? Too late to be thinking about that now,* I thought as I swam and pulled my way through the crevices.

What are you doing, Randolph? His voice had come from behind me.

I whirled around and began to make my descent back through the tunnel. *He was here, I knew it!* I thought as the water pushed me along. I swam out of the opening and into the waterfall pool. Whatever lay in the cave beneath the waterfall would have to wait. *Another time,* I thought.

Ben? I whispered in my mind, my body suspended in the blackness of the deep water. I listened and waited… expecting him to appear out of the darkness. No one was there.

I pulled myself out of the water and onto the grass that lined its banks. My body was glowing like a shimmery mist in the moonlight as I lay back and breathed in the night air. The night sky was clearing, the stars were brilliant, like thousands of pinholes in a black velvet blanket.

I lay there thinking about the light I had seen earlier. I was absolutely sure of two things: I had seen something and whatever—whoever—it was would be back. And now, I knew where they would be.

"Why would they be here? Why now?" I asked, thinking out loud.

Suddenly, I heard something. I sat straight up and strained my eyes and ears to pick up any sound or motion. *Yes,* I could hear muffled voices, and they were getting closer. Voices that appeared to be coming toward the falls. *Shit…shit…who else is crazy enough to be out in the middle of the night? Now, what do I do?* I thought, trying to weigh the options I had as the voices were getting more clear and closer. I quickly got to my feet, quietly gathered my shoes and clothes, wrapped them in my sweatshirt, and made my way to the base of the waterfall. Carefully stepping over the rocks that led to the ledge behind the falls. *Thank you, Lord…and Anna,* I thought.

I moved to the middle of the falls, pressing my body as close against the wall of wet rock as I could.

Christi, what's the big deal…you have as much right to be out here in the middle of the night as they do…get a grip. No, I remembered, *this is not Poppie's property. I was trespassing.*

"Liam, stop!" I heard a female voice say, as she started to laugh.

"Don't call me that, you know my name," a male voice responded.

I've heard those voices before. A cold chill ran through my body.

"Just one more kiss before we go in, please, Sariai. I'll do anything for you, you know I will."

Sariai. That had been the name Ben had used that night in the water. The night I had followed him into the ocean. I had been caught in some sphere of energy under the water. He was protecting me from the one that had tried to…I don't even know what she had tried to do…or what she had meant. I just remember hearing her say, *She's mine.* It was the night I discovered who—what—Ben really was.

I could see their silhouettes through the cascading water. They moved toward each other and kissed. I leaned forward, straining to hear what they were saying.

"This is so much better than before, can't we just stay like this? I mean those legs," he said as he ran his hands down her hips and thighs. "Those lips." He kissed her again.

His voice was of the one who had put up the opposition when Ben was pleading with the one he had referred to as *Father.*

"These will do for now, but soon we won't need humans. We'll have all the power we need." She took him by the hand as they walked toward the falls. "These shells won't be able to contain the power we'll have. Even Ion won't be able to stop us. I'll see to it. He'll come here because of her. But he won't be able to protect her from us. Not after…" Her words trailed off. He began kissing her neck. "Not as soon as we…" Her voice trailed off again.

"Soon, my love, but can't we just enjoy this while it lasts?" He wrapped his arms around her and kissed her again.

"What's this?" I heard him say as he pulled away from her. "It's a flashlight."

Shit, I thought. *How could I have been so careless not to have picked it up?*

"Someone's been here," she said. "They may still be here, look around. No one can know that we're here."

"It doesn't work, batteries are dead," I heard him say as I watched what was happening on the other side of the waterfall.

"There…all fixed." I could see the beam of light from the once-dead flashlight as he flicked it on and off as if admiring his handy work.

"The magic touch, and one whose hands that I love touching me." She moved even closer to him.

I stared through the flowing water as the flashlight lit up her face. I could see her clearly. Her soft, delicate features seemed to change as her tone changed. "Now, look around!" she commanded him.

He slowly flashed the beam of light over the pool of water as they scanned the surface. "No one is here," he said.

"Look around the waterfall." Her tone again was more of an order than a request.

"Just two starstruck lovers," he laughed as I saw the circular light he was carrying moving toward the rocks at the side of the waterfall. The rocks that lead to the ledge. The ledge where I was frozen in place.

You have to do something. I was trying to process everything that was happening and make some sense of it and trying not to breathe. *Concentrate...you can do this...concentrate.* It was what I would tell myself when I tried to keep my body from disappearing into a vapor-like state. Now, I needed it to happen. I stepped forward into the mist and spray that was created by the waterfall, letting its cool moistness soak my body. *Would it be enough?*

He was there, standing at the opening onto the ledge. I was motionless. Wanting to look down at my body to see if my mind—my will—was working, but I was too afraid to move. Knowing that at any moment, I would be discovered.

He took a step toward me on the ledge when suddenly he stopped, turned around, and stepped down the rocks toward the water. "There's nothing here," he said. They stood there for a moment at the edge of the falls, kissed a final time, then they dove into the water without another word.

I just stood there, breath escaping my lungs.

This is what Ben had meant when he said he was not the only one who had stayed behind. What could they have been talking about? They were planning something, but what? All these thoughts were running through my head. Suddenly I felt dizzy. Stepping back, I leaned against the wet rock wall behind me and closed my eyes.

"Go home, Christi," I heard him say.

"Ben?" I opened my eyes, expecting to see him standing there beside me.

"Go home." His voice was as clear as if he was right there with me.

They were the words he had spoken to me on the beach that night. *Was I just imagining it? Are you real, or are you just inside my mind?* I thought as I slowly, quietly made my way out from behind the waterfall. I looked around for him, hoping he would be standing by the water waiting for me. I stared at the pool, expecting to see two lights reflecting in the moonlight. I wondered if they would be able to sense my presence now that I was fully human and out in the open.

Nothing, no Ben…no lights. So many thoughts were running through my head as I walked around the pool of water. Picking up the once dead flashlight, I ran. I threw on my hat, stumbling, attempting to put on my clothes. Stopping only to take the time to put on my shoes.

I continued on to the trail that would lead me back to where I had tied Midnight. Occasionally, I would glance back at the waterfall that was becoming a little more visible now, in the darkness just before the dawn. Its white foamy brilliance cascaded over the mountain ledge. Everything seemed so normal.

I sighed in relief as I rounded the curve in the path, seeing that Midnight was there waiting for me. I ran him faster than I ever have. My heart was pounding in my chest. Closing the gate to the outer pasture, I again heard the distant howl of a wolf. It suddenly became perfectly clear that I was part of something much bigger than I had even let myself think. Something that, whether I wanted it or not,

I was now a part of. And that my life—and Ben's—would depend on finding out what that something was.

My body was shaking as I squeezed my heels into Midnight's sides. He responded as we sprinted across the field toward the barn.

The sun was beginning to come up.

Chapter Six

"Please be unlocked." I tried the passenger door of the rental car. It opened easily. Reaching in, I grabbed my iPod and earbuds that I had left in the front console. *What better way to escape my thoughts than listening to Adele.*

The lights were on in the kitchen, which meant Aunt Abby was already up having her coffee. I walked around to the back door, praying the screen door had been left unlocked. It had been. I let the door close quietly behind me, walked over, and pulled on the big wooden door.

"Shoot!" I sighed. It had not been.

"Aunt Abby!" I knocked and waited for her to cross the kitchen to the porch.

"What on earth are you doing out there this early?" I walked past her and into the kitchen. "Luvy, are you wet?"

"I went out to the car to get my music. I'm going to run this morning. The door must have accidentally locked behind me," I lied as I held up my iPod. "And I guess I got in a hurry when I was drying off after my shower," I lied again, looking down at my clothes.

I brushed past her walking over to the cabinet and picked out a cup, a thin-rimmed one, from the collection of mugs and cups that lined the shelves. I began to fill it from the fresh pot of coffee she had just finished making. I sat down at the table in the large farmhouse kitchen.

"Come sit and have a cup of coffee with me." I motioned to the chair across from me, hoping that changing the subject would work.

She knew, giving me that "Are you changing the subject?" look as only she could give. But she kept quiet as she walked over and sat across from me.

I spooned two sugars into my cup and reached for the creamer. "What are we going to do today? Go into town? Hike up to the lake?" I asked, trying to sound excited.

"I think we better wait to see what your mom might have planned." She took a sip from her cup.

"Why? Why can't we do what we want to do? She will control our whole week here if you let her." I shoved my chair back and walked around the table toward the stairs.

"Christi! Why do you get so upset over the smallest things anymore?"

I stopped at the foot of the stairs and waited. *Was she going to start lecturing me now?*

"Okay, we can do either of those things." Her tone had softened. "Why don't you decide?"

"Good morning, you two," I heard my mom say from the top of the stairs. She began to make her way down toward me. "I can smell the coffee from up here," she chirped.

The sound of her voice irritated me. *Aunt Abby was right, the smallest things.* "I think I'm going to go ahead and get my run in now." I turned away from the stairs and stepped toward the door.

"I think you should wait and see what Tom has found out," Aunt Abby said. "It may be dangerous for you to be out by yourself, Luvy." She was looking back and forth from my mom, then back to me.

"You're beginning to sound just like her, for Christ's sake. I'm not a kid anymore. Besides, Tom's already said it was okay." I sighed in disgust, rolling my eyes.

"Christi!" my mom exclaimed.

"I'm sorry I snapped at you, Aunt Abby, but Tom did say it was okay. Right, Mom?" I glared at her. "I'll be fine. I won't get off the main road. I'll just go to the T." I didn't wait for them to find another reason why I couldn't go.

"Luvy, don't you at least want to change your wet clothes?" I heard her say as I closed the door behind me.

I put on "Rolling in the Deep" and tried to lose myself in the words of the songs on my playlist. What usually worked was impossible as the thoughts of what had just happened at the waterfall were still running through my head. I was in the middle of something, and I had no idea what it was.

I made my way to the end of the driveway and onto the main road. Dew was glistening on the blades of grass. I decided to run east so I could catch a glimpse of the sun as it peaked through the valley openings below the mountain range.

Running to where the roads' *T* would be about three miles. It was a trip we had made on our way to town many times on our vacations here. There and back would help me keep pace with the training that I needed to make the track team. It was now my one *normal*. That would have to be what I focused on, my dream of a swimming scholarship was gone. I needed something that I could do where I could relieve some frustration and be in my own world where I could at least think. Running did that.

The darkness had faded, and now, the outline of the mountains was becoming clearer. They were so beautiful. Not in the same way as the sand and waves of the ocean were beautiful, but beautiful just the same. I ran along the deserted road, looking out over the land that spread to the base of the mountains on both sides. It was incredible.

How could people think that all this just happened...that there was some Big Bang somewhere in the universe and all this came to be? That the oceans and mountains and everything in between just evolved? How could you see the beauty in all of this and not believe that there is a God?

I knew I was kidding myself; those same people who believed in God would never think that Ben was real. Or that there could ever be life on another planet. Or that anything that had happened to me was real. I knew that God was real, and I knew what happened...happened. But how could I explain it to anyone?

I had not even been able to bring myself to tell Aunt Abby about what had happened while we were at the beach last spring, or what was still happening to me. How could I explain something that I did not even really understand myself?

"Quit thinking about it," I murmured and turned up the volume. *Set fire to the rain* rang in my ears.

I ran…looking out at the grasses swaying in the morning breeze. I imagined that they were ocean waves and that the occasional birds that popped up from the ground were dolphins; they were swimming along beside me. I smiled.

I could see it approaching in the distance. A pickup truck coming toward me. As it neared, the smell of hot oil and burning rubber filled the air.

The truck slowed and came to a stop beside me. It was Manny sitting in the driver's seat. As I removed my earbuds, I heard the passenger door close.

"Good morning, little lady." He nodded toward me.

Anna came around from the rear of the truck. "Can I run with you?" she asked with a big smile. "I won't slow you down, I promise, and I won't talk unless you want to."

"Is it okay?" he asked. They were both looking at me, waiting for my response.

"I'm training. I'm running all the way to the railroad tracks and back." I tried to sound discouraging. Thinking that would make a difference, hoping to deter her. Didn't seem to faze her.

"That's fine. I can do that."

"Great, see you girls back at the ranch then," her dad said as he waved his hand out the window.

"Bye, Dad." She waved back. The rusted out old truck lurched forward and pulled away.

I stood there looking at her. Her hands on her hips, she was bending from side to side. "What? Aren't you supposed to loosen up?" she smiled.

I put my music back on, turned, and headed toward the tracks. We had not run a mile when I could tell she was beginning to struggle. *I knew it,* I thought, but I was not going to slow my pace for her. *She could keep up…or not.* I turned the volume higher.

Maybe I was too hard on her, after all, she has no clue what was going on. I slowed my pace a little so that she could catch up. We ran side by side, only glancing at each other when an occasional car or truck would pass.

We passed a dirt lane that was fenced and gated. Anna stopped and began pointing, saying something. I took my earbuds off. "That's where Liam and his family lives." She paused, catching her breath. "His dad's the vet, you know, he takes care of all the animals at the farm."

"Liam?" I asked. I knew who she was talking about.

"Yes, gorgeous, hot Liam," she laughed as she fanned her face.

"Do you even know him? Or anything about him?" I looked at her, knowing the answer. I had just seen him at the waterfall and knew that who Liam was, who he had been, was not who she thought he was.

"Not much, I really don't know anyone yet. I just know that he's been nice to me when I've seen him," she answered.

"Does he have a girlfriend?" I was fishing to find out about the girl that was with him at the waterfall. Who the human girl had been.

"Girlfriend! I don't think so. Why, are you interested in him? You don't even know him, do you?" She had a puzzled look on her face.

"I remember Liam. I've been coming here with my mom and stepdad for years you know. Have you seen him with someone? If he's all that hot, he must have girls swarming all over him?" I pushed, trying to see if she knew or had seen anything.

"No, not really, I haven't seen him with anyone. Just kids at school. But I've only seen him a couple of times. He's nice, and hot...did I mention he was hot?" She laughed. Her swooning over him made me smile. "His family owns almost all the property from here into town, all the way to the waterfall." She made a sweeping motion with her hand.

"The waterfall?" A chill ran down my spine.

"Yes, remember I said that when we were there." She pointed along the field. "The creek runs from the waterfall and under the bridge that is just ahead of us."

We stood for a moment at the end of the drive and looked out over the land as the sunlight was shining through the valley. We couldn't see the house from here, just the roofs of the barns in the distance at the end of the long lane that was lined with huge evergreen trees.

We turned and jogged along the paved road closing the distance to the bridge that she had pointed to moments before. We stopped on the bridge and looked at the creek bed below. The shallow water rippled out of the big metal culvert pipe, where the creek water ran underneath the surface of the road. Running over and through the rocks as it made its way to the river that flowed through the edge of the town just a few miles away. We started to turn away when I heard something. It was a faint whimper...like a dog's whimper. I stopped and listened. *Yes*, I thought, *it is a dog.*

"Anna, do you hear that?" I looked down at the pipe, then back at her. I made my way down the side of the road and looked inside the tube.

"What are you doing? I don't hear anything." She was making her way down the side of the culvert also.

It was too dark inside the large drainage pipe to see anything clearly. The whimper was now a moan. I couldn't see it, but I could hear it. I felt for my phone. "Shit! No signal…that figures," I said. I looked disgustingly at the screen that did not have a single bar showing. "Can you get a signal?" I yelled at her as I began to make my way the rest of the way down the steep incline to the base of the creek.

"I don't even have a phone," she said. "Wait, I can hear it too." She slid down the side of the creek bank. The whimpers grew louder as they echoed in the metal pipe.

"It's a dog," I said. "Come here, boy." I moved, half-crawling into the culvert trying to straddle the water that ran through the center of it. "Where are you? Are you okay?" As if I was expecting it to answer me. I saw it, laying about halfway inside. I slowly moved toward the dog. It made no motion to get up.

"Christi, stop, that's not a dog. I think it's a wolf," I heard Anna say.

"It's okay, we're here to help you." I ignored her as I walked closer to the animal that was now just a few feet away from me.

"Christi, it's hurt and could be dangerous. Let's go get help." She was talking, but I wasn't listening.

It was dark in the pipe, the sun had not yet come up enough to shed much light inside. As I inched closer, I could see that there was something attached to the dog's leg, it looked like a rope of some kind.

What is it? I thought. "It's caught on something," I called back to her as I kept inching toward it.

It didn't move as I stood over the wounded animal. The whimpering stopped. It looked up at me as if it knew that I was there to help it.

"Oh my god!" I realized what it was hooked to. It was a trap. One of its front legs was caught in this metal clamp that was attached to a chain, a chain that led outside the drainpipe.

"Anna, come help me," I yelled at her.

"What in the world?" she whispered as she made her way behind me inside the drainpipe.

I slowly moved around the animal, following the chain outside the drainpipe, looking for where it was connected. It had been welded to a stake and driven deep into the ground. I pulled on it. It didn't budge.

"Help me!" I yelled to Anna, who was still standing there looking at the trapped animal.

"That's a wolf, look at it. That's not a dog, and it's probably the one that has been killing the cattle, we can't just let it loose." Her eyes were darting back and forth from me to the wounded animal.

"It is not a wolf! What's killing the cattle, I mean." I kept pulling on the stake. "And we don't know that this is a wolf either."

"Look at it, it is a wolf!" she yelled.

"Fine, then leave and go get help!" I was mad. Mad that she was not listening to me, mad that someone had done this, mad that we were in this godforsaken place where there was no cell service.

I turned and walked back toward where it lay. "Will you let me look at you?" I whispered as I inched toward it, knowing full well how dangerous a wounded dog, let alone a wolf could be. It made no movement as I knelt down beside it. My eyes followed the chain to the end of the clamp; it had cut deep into its leg.

Suddenly, it raised its head and growled a low growl. I fell backward. In an instant, it was on its feet and standing over me...teeth snarling.

"Christi!" Anna screamed.

"It's okay. It's okay...I'm not going to hurt you. And you are not going to hurt me." I looked him in the eyes, trying not to let the fear show in my voice.

I could see it more clearly now as it stood there, out of the shadows. The dim light framed the outline of its body. Its reddish-gray fur shining in the light. Its green eyes stared back at me. Its foot had been cut severely by the trap. The bone was sticking out, blood was still coming from the wound.

"Who did this to you?" I asked softly. Lying there on my back, I reached out to touch the animal, forgetting that with one bite he could take off my hand.

We watched the wound as I touched it. "Wow," Anna whispered. It began to glow as if a light was shining on it. We looked on as it healed itself. The bone pushed itself into place, the skin came together, fur now covering where the cut had been. The hard metal blades of the trap were still there, yet somehow, there was no cut, not even any blood. The wolf backed away from me, lay down in the same spot where he had been, and began licking where the wound had been.

"Did I just see that? What just happened?" Anna murmured.

I felt dizzy as I sat up. "It's dark in here, I don't know what you think you saw, but..."

"No, it's not that dark. I was standing right here. I saw what I saw. What was that you just did?"

I knew the feeling of your mind trying to rationalize something you had just seen. We should have left and gone for help in the beginning. I wished we had. This would not have happened, she would not have witnessed what she just saw. But she had, and now I couldn't just leave him there… chained.

"Okay, we are going to try this again, and you are going to help me," I said to her as I stood slowly.

I knelt beside him again, feeling my way down the chain to the metal blades. I could see the lever that released the pressure of the trap. I tried to push on it. It didn't move.

"Anna!" I looked at her, changing my position so I could put more weight on it.

She came closer and knelt beside me just as the lever gave a little, but it clamped back into place. The wolf moaned and snapped at me, causing us both to lose our balance. Anna and I both fell backward.

"I'm sorry, I'm sorry," I whispered, never taking my eyes off him. We got to our feet and stood there looking down at the mighty animal. His eyes seemed to soften; suddenly he looked helpless and vulnerable.

"Okay, we are going to have just one chance at this," I said to Anna, and to the wolf. "When we push on this lever…you are going to pull your leg out. You hear me? When we push, you pull." He made no other move to resist us.

We positioned ourselves, bracing our legs as best we could to put as much pressure on the trap's lever as possible.

"Okay…you ready? Let's do this."

Part Two

Chapter Seven

I looked at her as we placed our hands one on top of the other and began to push as hard as we could on the disk-shaped lever.

"Push, Anna! And you"—I looked the wolf in the eyes—"you...pull, damn it...pull." I pushed so hard, it felt as if my eyes were about to pop out. Suddenly the trap opened slightly. He was free, and just like that...he ran out of the drainage pipe. The trap snapped back into place.

"Without even a thank-you," Anna said.

We looked at each other and laughed as we sat there, taking a moment to breathe, letting what had just happened sink in.

"Are you an angel?" Her voice was quiet as she broke the silence.

"What?" I laughed at her, shaking my head, not sure that I had heard her correctly.

"I believe in angels, you know, my mom's one. I know she watches over my dad and me." I sat there in silence, still holding the chain that had been a death trap. "It's all right, you don't have to talk about it. I won't tell anyone," she said softly, putting her arm around my shoulder.

"I feel like there is a bribe coming. As long as I go to the open house with you, right?" I tried to make light of what had just happened. What we had both just witnessed. Not even knowing myself what had taken place.

"I'm not trying to be funny, and I don't want anything from you. I just want you to know it's okay, and that I'm here for you if you ever want or need to talk." The words she was speaking were so sincere that my emotions began to overwhelm me.

"I'm not sure what I am, Anna, but I am definitely not an angel." I looked over at her as a tear spilled down my cheek.

The thought that I might finally have someone I could talk to. Someone who would not judge me or try to rationalize everything that had happened. Someone who could hear what I was saying and not twist and turn it to fit their idea of normal. Someone who would actually believe all the events that had taken place. Someone who could think that I could be an angel...would surely believe everything else.

"Whatever it is, it's going to be okay," she said softly.

I stood, drying my eyes. My hands were still shaking, "Thank you, Anna."

I looked down at the trap as I carried it out to the stake where it was anchored. Blood and fur were stuck on the blades as a reminder of what a death instrument it was meant to be.

"Not today." I threw the trap on the ground. We rinsed our hands in the cold, rippling water of the creek and made our way up the steep incline to the road.

We ran on the deserted road, with just the sounds of our shoes, squeaking as they made contact with the pavement, and the rhythmic pattern of our breathing. Occasionally glancing out, scanning the open land on both sides of the road for any signs of movement. Hoping to catch a glimpse of the animal that we had just set free and somehow still trying to make sense of what had just taken place. I knew something had been happening inside me. I could feel it. It was almost a burning sensation inside my body. But how could I explain it?

I looked down at my hands as if they were foreign to my body and not even a part of me. Out in the distance, there was only the grass swaying in the breeze. No sign of any wolves.

"He's long gone." Anna broke the silence. "My dad says they mostly come out at night, so he is probably in a safe place thanking his lucky stars that you came by this morning."

"About what happened back there…" I started to explain.

"I meant it when I said that I wouldn't talk about it unless you wanted to."

I didn't look at her, but I knew what she must have been thinking. The same thing that I had felt when I realized that I couldn't say anything about Ben. *That the impossible had become a reality.*

We ran without any more conversation as the intersection came into view. Just then I saw motion out the corner of my eye. I stopped and instinctively grabbed Anna by the arm.

"What? It's just the train." She laughed.

As we ran along the road, I began to tell her a story Poppie had shared with me on one of my first visits here. A story about him and his friend who would "hobo" the train. Meaning that they would time the distance perfectly and jump into one of the open rail cars as it passed. Then ride it into town. *It was such an adrenalin rush*, he had said. It was something they had done more than once.

The trains distance was beginning to close as we approached the T where the road we were on intersected the main road into town. Left would take you into town, the right would take you along the river to the main highway.

I looked at each car in the train as it snaked along the side of the road. "I think I can do it. I think I can jump on the train, just like Poppie did."

"Haven't you had enough excitement for one day?" She looked at me like I was crazy.

"There, that one is open. Help me count...one thousand one...one thousand two..."

"Christi, are you crazy? Those are just old tales your Poppie told you. He never jumped on no train, and he certainly would not let you even think about it, let alone do it. So stop it!" She grabbed my arm.

I ignored her. I tried to estimate the timing and the distance of the one boxcar whose big metal door I could see had been left open.

We stood at the crossroad, waiting for the approaching train. As the engine got closer and closer, my heart started to beat faster and faster. My timing would have to be perfect. I would have to judge the speed of the train just right to make the jump successful. There was a small pull-off area on the other side of where the roads intersected. The tracks were several feet lower. I would have to time it perfectly, then make a running jump for it.

The sound of the rattling of the train echoed against the quietness of the morning, as the engine rolled past us. The clanging of the rails, the sound of metal against metal filled the air.

"You can't be serious?" Anna yelled.

Over and over in my mind, I counted the seconds that passed from one train car to the next. The open car was approaching quickly. *Three cars...that's when you need to run*, I thought.

"Come on, let's head back." Anna reached out and pulled on my arm. The cars rattled by.

Five...

"Christi!"

*Four...three...*I ran straight for the train that was just a few yards on the other side of the pavement.

"Stop!" I heard her scream.

I stopped just inches from the edge of the grass that lined the embankment on the side of the road. My heart was racing. I could not only feel, but hear, the pounding in my chest.

The rail car with the open door passed by us. I stood there, frozen in place as the train rattled by me just a few feet away. Letting the reality sink in. *If I had jumped, I would have jumped too soon.*

Suddenly everything that had happened on our trip to the beach all those months ago flashed before me like a movie…all the feelings…all the emotion came rushing back like a flood.

"Are you done now?" I heard her say as I watched the last car move farther away down the tracks. I turned and walked back to where I had left her.

"You didn't really think I was going to jump, did you?" She just shook her head as she stood there looking at me. I smiled, put on my music, and jogged past her, not waiting for a response. The sun was warm against my back as we made our way back toward the ranch. I looked out over the distance, not sure what I was hoping to see if anything.

It was a Jeep that I spotted, not a wolf. It was coming down the long dirt lane that we had passed earlier, the land owned by the Bakers, Liam's family.

It stopped at the end of the driveway and seemed to be waiting for us. *This could be interesting*, I thought as we were nearing the silver and black open-topped Jeep.

"Hey, Anna," he yelled over the roar of the engine of the open-range vehicle.

"Hey, Liam." She smiled, walking over toward the passenger door.

"Stop drooling," I whispered. "And remember what I said."

"Who's your friend?" He looked at me as if he may have heard my remark. *Of course, he did*, I thought.

"This is Christi. I thought you two knew each other?" She looked at him and back to me.

"It has been a while, I am sure Liam knows a lot of girls. It's okay." I never took my eyes off him. She turned to give me that look.

"Where are you headed? Want a ride?" he asked. He leaned over and opened the passenger-side door.

"Sure" and "No, thank you" were our simultaneous responses.

"Anna, I thought we were running." My eyes were still fixed on him.

She turned and walked back to where I was standing. "You are only here for a couple of weeks," she whispered. "Me, I have to live here. I haven't made any friends yet, and I'm not going to pass up this opportunity. Besides, look at him." She winked. "You can come or not," she spoke quietly, using my words.

Part of me wanted to just let her go, but I knew I couldn't let her go alone. Knowing that Liam was not at all the guy that Anna thought he was. Or who he used to be. He was not the guy anyone of us thought he was. Not any longer. And until I knew for sure what he was involved in—what they were planning—she was in danger.

"Wait up." I walked over to the Jeep, opened the back-passenger door, and climbed in. He looked at me in his rearview mirror, shifted the Jeep into drive, and pulled out onto the paved road.

"You guys going to the open house at the school tomorrow?" He was all smiles and charm, looking over at Anna.

"Christi's not going to be here for long. She's not going to school here as I thought. I'm trying to convince her to come, though. Just to meet everyone. But I will be there for sure." She smiled back at him.

"Well, that's a shame," he said in a sarcastic tone as he turned to look at me. "I think you would like it here. Besides, it's going to be a wild summer. Sure you don't want to be a part of it?" It was like he was teasing me, baiting me almost.

I looked for any sign that he may have known that I was there at the falls last night. Any clue in his demeanor that he thought I knew something.

"You're only here for a couple of weeks, right?" Anna asked, knowing the answer.

"Two weeks is a long time. I'll be here long enough," I said, never taking my eyes off him as he shifted his attention to Anna.

"We are also having a big bonfire at the waterfall tomorrow night, everyone from school will be there. You two should come, it would be a chance to get to know some of us, make some new friends." There was smugness in his tone as he looked back at me.

I didn't wait for Anna to respond. "Yes, we will be there. I do want to get to know some of you better."

Anna turned and gave me a look as if I were trying to come on to her boyfriend or something.

"It'll be fun, won't it, Anna?" I tried to smooth it over. Knowing how my quick accepting of his invitation probably looked to her.

"Great! I'll look forward to it then. You were heading home, right?" he asked as he slowed approaching the drive. Anna shook her head.

The ride had been brief, but it had been an opportunity to observe him. Hopefully, the invitation to the bonfire would lead to learning more about what he and his friend were up to and what really might be going on with them. What it had to do with Ben…and me.

I looked back out of the open Jeep. No sign of the wolf. Just a few bison that had strayed out in the morning sun to warm themselves. He was out there somewhere, and I knew that our paths would somehow cross again.

We turned into the driveway that led to the house. As we neared the circular drive, I could see that there was a car parked in front of the house, one I didn't recognize.

Liam suddenly seemed to be nervous. "I'll let you out here." He stopped the Jeep short of the house.

"Something wrong?" I asked, looking for his reaction.

His expression never changed as he shifted anxiously in the driver's seat. "I just remembered I left something back at the house. Sorry, I have to go," he said. His eyes darting from the house to the parked car.

We opened the doors and slowly got out of the Jeep. Anna leaned in the open window. "Okay. Thanks, Liam." She stepped away, waving as he began to back toward the entrance to the barn. "See you at school tomorrow," she yelled to him.

"That was weird," she said as we walked down the drive toward the house.

"There are a lot of things that are weird. Welcome to the new normal."

I looked at the license plates on the car that was parked in the drive in front of the house.

US government license plates.

Chapter Eight

"Aren't you going to come in?" I stopped at the bottom of the steps waiting for Anna. She was still just standing in the driveway, staring at the plates on the back of the car.

"No, I have to go too. I need to find my dad." She suddenly turned and ran toward the barn.

Now, who's acting weird? I thought as I stood there and watched as she closed the gate behind her, disappearing into the barn.

I looked at the car that was not at all familiar to me. *Maybe it belonged to Dr. Baker. Could explain why Liam acted so weird. But Government plates?* I asked myself, making my way up the steps to the big front door of the farmhouse.

I heard them talking as I closed the door behind me and walked into the dining room. They were sitting around the big wooden table. Fresh coffee had been poured, and warm cinnamon rolls were on a platter in its center. They turned to look at me as I entered the room. My mom, Aunt Abby, and the man sitting with them.

"There you are, Luvy," Aunt Abby stood and walked over to me as I moved closer to the table. "You remember Detective Baker, don't you?" She took my arm and led me to the table.

The man stood and held out his hand. I recognized him to be the man I had seen at the beach that night, the night that Ben and Mr. Carlton had gone into the water. The night when everything changed. He was the one who had come to the house after I had gotten home from the hospital and questioned me about Ben.

I ignored his hand. "What is he doing here?" I asked, looking from Aunt Abby to my mom and back to the Detective who was still standing there with his hand out-stretched. "Are you here about Ben? Do you know where he is? Is he okay?" The questions came pouring out of my mouth.

"That's what I would like to ask you. Have you heard from him?" He pulled his hand back to his side.

I walked over to the desk and plugged my cell phone into the charger. "I haven't seen or heard from him since I talked to you in South Carolina, and I have nothing more to tell you, so why are you here?" I asked sharply.

"Christi! Don't be so rude," my mom said. "Detective Baker is a relative of our neighbors. As a matter of fact, Dr. Baker is his brother."

"That still amazes me. It's a small world, isn't it?" Aunt Abby inserted.

"It's quite all right, Mrs. Snyder," he said. He never took his attention away from me. "Like I was just telling your mom and Mrs. Collins, I am visiting my brother's family, but that's not the reason I'm here. I'm here on official business." He stepped back and picked up a black folder that was laying on the table. "I'm looking for these two people." He took two photos from the folder and handed them to my mom.

"Who are they?" Her concern showing on her face.

I slowly walked over to the table and looked over her shoulder, staring down at the images in the photos. Even though I had no clue who they were, I had seen one of them. The girl in the picture was the same girl who had been with Liam at the waterfall last night. Even though it had been dark, it was her. I was absolutely sure of it.

"Their names are Nick Abbott and Audrey Langley. They have been missing from their homes in Surfside. It's been over a week since their family or friends have heard from them. We received a report that they may have been seen in this area. So, if by chance, you see them, please contact me as soon as possible."

I heard what he was saying, but my eyes were glued to the images in front of me. My mind was spinning. It seemed like minutes passed before he broke the silence.

"I've not seen them, but I'll certainly ask around," my mom answered. "Have you checked in town? Or go by the school tomorrow, maybe some of the kids have seen them around." She laid the photo on the table in front of her.

"Yes, ma'am. I'm heading there now. And you?" He stood there looking at me. "You've not seen them?"

I was still staring at the photos in front of me. My hands were beginning to shake.

"Christi just arrived here, she's not had time to even get out yet," my mom explained.

"She was just out. Weren't you?" he asked, stepping around his chair. "Did you see anything unusual?"

"No!" I quickly clasped my hands together to stop them from shaking, hoping he had not noticed.

"You'll be sure to call me if you do. Won't you?" he asked.

"Of course she will…we will," Aunt Abby answered for me.

"Well, thank you, ladies, for your time. Remember to always use caution when you are out and about. My advice is to not go out alone. But if you do, stick to the main roads, and the marked trails." He pushed the chair back under the table, picked up the folder that was laying in front of him and placed the photos inside. "And thank you for the coffee."

"You're welcome, and thank you." My mom walked past him to open the door.

Aunt Abby stood. "We'll be extra careful when we're out. And we'll keep those kids in our prayers," she said softly.

"Oh, I do have one more thing." He paused at the door. "If by chance you do hear from Ben, you be sure to let him know that I still have some questions for him. Good day, ladies."

I could hear the sound of his footsteps on the front porch as my mom closed the door behind him and walked back to the table.

"Honey, you're shaking, and you're white as a ghost. Here, sit down," she said as she pulled out one of the big padded chairs. I didn't resist. I sat down, laying my head down on the wooden table.

"I don't feel so good." I suddenly felt sick.

"Here, let me get you some water, Luvy." Aunt Abby headed toward the kitchen, returning with a glass of ice water. She set it down on the table in front of me.

"Don't worry, Luvy. I'm sure those kids are fine, and they'll find them soon," Aunt Abby said softly, stroking my hair.

"I think you are just dehydrated from your run," my mom chimed in. "Maybe, you should rest a while after you finish your water."

"I think I will go up and lie down." I stood, wobbling, trying to steady myself. "I'm okay, I'm okay," I reassured both of them as they both reached for me.

I picked up the glass of water and headed up the staircase.

"I'll check on you in a bit," Aunt Abby said.

I didn't answer. I just continued up the stairs, and down the hall to my bedroom...to the room that I slept in when I came here. It would never be my room. I closed the door behind me and leaned my head back against its solidness.

The girl from the waterfall was the girl in the photo. Her image kept replaying over and over in my head. He said her name was Audrey. Liam had called her Sariai. That was the name Ben had used for the one in the water that night. The one whose voice had said, *She's mine.*

I shivered remembering the fear I felt when she had spoken those words. Now these two missing people were from Surfside, close to where all of it had happened. Showing up here. *What is the connection? Was the same thing happening all over again?*

"Oh, I'm so confused," I said out loud as I kicked off my shoes, took off my sweatshirt, threw it on the floor, and laid across the bed.

I rolled over and stared at the ceiling. I could smell the scent of the wolf on my hands. I looked at them, stretched my arms out, reaching them toward the ceiling. Hands that were normal yet had somehow healed the wound the wolf had suffered. *How can I ever make sense of any of it?*

"Ben, I need you," I whispered as I rolled over on my side and curled my legs to my chest. *I'll lie here just for a little while*, I thought, closing my eyes.

Sleep came, and so did the dreams. I was submerged in some sort of container. My lungs were filling up with water. Not the salty taste of ocean water—it was cold, fresh, clean water. I was caught in the same cylinder, water was pouring in from the top with such force that I could only struggle against the weight of it. Fighting, needing air, yet not needing it. I knew I had to find a different way out. Swimming upward was not an option, so I began to swim down...down, down, my lungs were burning. *Keep going, you're almost there*, I told myself, not knowing where *there* was or even if there was a way out. I just kept swimming down. All of a sudden, the cylinder made a sharp turn. I began swimming upward again, following the air bubbles that were escaping from my nose. Just as the last bit of air escaped my lungs, I burst through the surface. Air flooded my being. I looked around trying to get my bearings, pulling myself up and out of the water onto the hard, wet rock floor.

I was inside some kind of rock formation. *A cave*, I thought. A beam of light was streaming from the top of the cave as dust particles danced in the rays, and rainbows were being formed by the mist. My eyes began to adjust to the darkness. I could see ledges of rock jutting out from the sides of the cavern that I found myself in. I looked around for a way out. There was none. The sides of the cavern were steep, and the ledges were too far apart for me to try to climb out. It would be impossible. The only way out was the way I had gotten in—through the cylinder. I stood there in the damp darkness and listened to the sound I was hearing…a constant loud roar. I recognized the familiar sound of rushing water. I was behind, inside the waterfall, and there was only one way out. Exhausted, I lay down on the wet hardness of the cave floor. *I'll lie here just for a little while,* I thought.

It was the pounding on the door that woke me. "Luvy, are you okay? Luvy, the door's stuck." Aunt Abby sounded frantic.

I sat up on the side of the bed. "I'm coming, I'm coming," I yelled back at her. I stood beside my bed, looking at the big wooden door across the floor of the bedroom. My mind was trying to separate my dreams from reality.

"You had better get that." I heard his voice coming from the other side of the room. I turned around, expecting that the sound I heard was in my head, just as it had been all the times before.

"Ben?" I whispered, tears beginning to well up in my eyes.

"Luvy?" Aunt Abby knocked again.

"I'm coming, just give me a minute," I shouted, not looking away from Ben.

I walked over to the window where he was standing. "Are you for real, or am I dreaming?" He reached his hand out for mine. I slowly stretched my hand as he took it in his. My heart was racing as he pulled me closer to him.

"I told you I would find you." He softly stroked my hair.

The creaking of the door opening startled me. I dropped Ben's hands and whirled around to see Aunt Abby stumble into the room as the door flung open.

"Oh my goodness!" She gasped as she caught herself on the side of the bed. "Wow! Luvy, I've been knocking and knocking. The door must have been stuck or something." She looked back at it. "I was getting worried. Are you sure you are okay?" She began walking toward us.

"Aunt Abby, you can't just burst into my room...I'm fine." I rushed over to her and grabbed her by the arm, trying to lead her back across the room. Knowing I would have to explain why Ben was standing there in my bedroom.

"You've been up here for a while, I was getting concerned, and then when the door wouldn't open and when you didn't answer." She was rambling...trying to explain. "I was worried about you." She reached up and touched my face.

"It's okay," I reassured her.

"It's a beautiful day out." She looked toward the window...the window where Ben was still standing. The sun was beaming through the sheer curtain. "I thought we would hike the trail by the lake this afternoon like you wanted. Not too far, maybe the short trail, only if you feel like it though?"

It was as if she was oblivious to him. As if she didn't even see him. I walked over to the window, stood beside Ben, and pulled the white sheer curtain away from the pane. I let it fall back into place and turned to face her. She was still standing there, smiling that loving smile that she reserved just for me.

She does not see him, just like she did not see him at the airport. How can that be? I thought.

"I would love to do that," I smiled back. "I'll be down in a little bit."

"Great, don't be too long. We want to take advantage of the sunshine. Maybe Poppie can even go out with us." She raised her eyebrows excitedly, closing the door behind her.

I stood there for a moment, then slowly turned toward Ben. "I know I'm going crazy, but did that just happen?"

He looked at me, put his hand on my shoulder, and tipped my face up until our eyes met. "You can be sure of three things, you are not crazy, you are not dreaming, and this." He pulled me to him and kissed me. Gently at first, then I wrapped my arms around him and kissed him. I kissed him like I had wanted to ever since he left me that day. Like I had kissed him in my dreams. Like I didn't want it to end. I laid my head on his chest. I could feel his heartbeat. It felt good. I felt a peace and calmness I had not felt since we left the dunes that day. I didn't want to let go of him, or for this feeling to end. Because letting go could mean he could leave again.

Minutes passed before he spoke. "We can't stay like this forever, you know," he said as if he knew what I was thinking.

"Why not?" I tried not to move a muscle.

"Well, your aunt will for sure be back to check on you," he smiled.

His comment jolted me back to reality if only for a moment. I leaned back to look at him.

"Aunt Abby? Why didn't she see you? And that's not the first time that that's happened, you know. She didn't see you at the airport either. When you ran into me. Why is that? Why can't she see you?"

He leaned forward and brushed his lips lightly across mine. "The question is not why she *can't* see me. The question is, why you *can*?"

Chapter Nine

"What does that even mean?" I pulled away from him and stepped back so that I could look at him. "Why does everything have to be a riddle of some kind? Why can't you just tell me the truth? I want to know, tell me what is going on, Ben."

Stepping around me, he walked over to the nightstand where I had placed the box...his box. He picked it up, sat down on the side of the bed, and slowly opened it. Taking out its contents, one by one, looking at each of the items before placing them on the bed beside him. He sat there staring at the one final piece remaining in the box. It was the frame I had put the picture of him and his family in.

Stuck to the corner of it was the note that read: *I'm counting on you to bury the past for me, but it will remain forever in our hearts.*

I could see the emotion that was beginning to well up inside him. I walked over and knelt in front of him.

"I feel like I am losing them," he whispered. "They're not the part of my past I wanted to forget." Tears began to spill down his cheeks. "There are times now that I can't even remember what they look like. I don't think I can stop it from happening." The sadness in his voice was heartbreaking.

I stood and wrapped my arms around him as the tears that had been building in both of us began to stream down our faces.

"You won't forget, you won't let yourself. And I won't let you," I reassured him. "I'll always be here to remind you. I want to help you, but to do that I have to understand what is happening." I felt his body trembling. "You have to tell me."

"Telling you will only put you in more danger." His tone changed suddenly as he stood and began to place the items back inside the box.

"No, my not knowing is what is putting me in danger." His answer was not good enough. I stood in front of him. He closed the box and put it back in the spot it had been on the nightstand.

He took my hands in his. "Come sit with me," he whispered.

"No, I don't want to sit down—I want to know what happened to me that night in the water. I want to know where you have been. I want to know about Sariai." I wanted him to know what I knew. "She's here you know... of course, you know. Were you there last night? It was you that I heard wasn't it?" I waited for him to answer. He sat there looking at me. "Why is she here, Ben? What does she want with me? And those two missing people. That girl,

Audrey…it's *her*…Sariai. She's her somehow. I saw her, you know, she was at the waterfall when—"

He raised my hands to his lips and gently kissed them. Softly touching his lips to each of my fingers, first one and then the other.

"Stop! I can't think or talk when you are doing that." I tried to sound like I wanted him to quit, but not wanting him to stop.

"Good, then don't think…just feel." His lips continued from my hand to my arm, down my arm to my neck. A chill ran down my body; his lips touched my cheek and then found mine.

Suddenly nothing else mattered. All the worry, all the anxiety, all the questions didn't matter. I had felt this sensation before, the tingling, the butterflies fluttering in my stomach. My heart felt like it would beat out of my chest. It was the same feeling that I had when he kissed me on the dunes that day. The last time that we had been together. He pulled away, leaving me standing there, my eyes still closed.

"I know you want to know everything, but some things are more dangerous for you to know right now," he said as he ran his fingers across my lips.

"That makes no sense. How can I protect myself if I don't know who or why I even need protecting?" I was frustrated and confused at the same time. I turned away from him and walked toward the window. "Actually, I do know from who…Sariai, she's here for me, isn't she? I heard her say that. And you, you are in danger too," I walked back over to the side of the bed. "I can't lose you, not when you have just come back."

He cupped my face in his hand. I leaned against it and gently kissed the palm of his hand.

"What does she want with me, Ben?" I looked at him, his expression had not changed. "It's power she wants, isn't it? From what I heard them say, it sounds like that to me."

"Them? Who else are you talking about?" His stance suddenly stiffened, and his expression changed to concern. He walked over to the window, pulling aside the sheer as if he were looking for something. The sun cast a shadow across his face.

"It was Liam. Well…I'm not sure that it was Liam exactly, but that's who was with her at the waterfall last night. His family owns the property right next to here. It looked like Liam, but his voice was someone else's. I remember the voice Ben, it was another voice that I heard in the water that night. The one who argued with you. I'll never forget his voice."

He stood there in silence, how vulnerable he suddenly seemed to be…how normal. I walked over and touched his arm.

"You need to promise me that you'll stay away from the waterfall." He never turned to look at me. He just kept staring out the window.

"O…K…and maybe I'll understand why, if you explain it to me. What's going on? You know that I need to know. I have to be able to protect myself. That detective is here too. The one that questioned me in South Carolina. He was here this morning. Asking about a couple of people who are missing from there. He had a photo—it's all connected some way, isn't it?" I sighed. "Ben, the girl in the picture was who was with Liam at the waterfall. Yet, it wasn't either one of them, not really, was it?" My voice was shaking. "Oh my god! I'm not even making any sense." I threw my hands up in frustration. "You have to tell me, please tell me something," I pleaded with him.

"You're right," he turned to look at me. "It is time for you to know some things."

"No, not just some things…everything."

"You know your aunt is waiting for you," he said, looking for a reason for me to stop my questioning. "She'll be calling for you any second."

"You're not going to get off that easy." I took his hand as we walked over and again sat on the side of the bed. "Besides, you are not getting rid of me." My voice broke with emotion.

He reached out and tucked a strand of my hair behind my ear. Just that simple gesture sent a tingling down my body. "Why would I want to?"

"Don't do that, I told you I can't think," I whispered, gently laying my other hand on top of his.

He looked me in the eyes. "She…Sariai is here because of you." His tone was soft and gentle. "She wants you. And she knows I'll do whatever it takes to stop her. She thinks that she can use you to get to me. She's right."

"Me, why? What could she want from me? How could I possibly be a threat to her?" I shook my head, confused.

He stroked my hand. "You truly don't know just how special you are, do you?"

"Special! It sounds like I am on her most wanted list. I guess if that makes me special." I forced a smile. I knew that what he was saying was dangerous and that our lives may depend on my understanding of what he was trying to tell me.

"Do you trust me?" he asked.

"Yes, you know, I do. I want to understand, and if I am putting you in danger, then you need to stay away from me." A tear spilled out and began to run down my cheek.

"I'm not going anywhere," he whispered softly. "You are right, this has to be dealt with...now." He wiped the tear away that had made its way to the edge of my chin.

"You remember that day at the airport? The day when fate brought you to me." He stood and walked over to the window.

I laughed sarcastically. "I remember the day that a moron ran into me and dumped my coffee all over me. I remember that TSA officer looking at us as if we were terrorists or something." I walked over to the window and stood beside him. I took his hand in mine, smiling as I recalled the awkward moment.

He squeezed my hand. "If falling for a princess makes me a moron, then that's okay with me." We both looked down at the bracelet that had brought us together that day. "But...it wasn't me."

I stared blankly at him. "It wasn't you what? Where? At the airport?"

"It wasn't me who bumped into you that day."

I shook my head in confusion. "What? Wait...yes it was, you...ran...into...me!" I was emphatic.

"No, it was Sariai. She was the reason I was there; to stop her. But fate stepped in that day. You were the one that stopped her."

I could hear him, and even though nothing he was saying was making sense, I knew if I trusted him, I was going to have to believe he was telling me the truth.

"Stop her from what? How? You were the only one there." I was trying to rationalize what he was saying, the events of that day swirled in my head.

"I was the only one that you saw," he said. "But, Sariai was there."

My mind was trying to process what he was telling me. "So I could see you, but I couldn't see her." I paused. "And just now, Aunt Abby couldn't see you. She didn't see you that day at the airport either. How can that be?" It was all becoming a blur. I stood there waiting for him to answer. "And don't you even say it's because I'm special." He smiled. "I'm serious. Can you control who is able to see you?" I asked.

His smile quickly faded. "You are the one thing that I can't figure out. I can control everyone else, but not you," he whispered. "I think that when she vapored-through you, you were somehow able to absorb some of her power." He walked a few steps away from me. "That somehow, you became a part of her, and she became a part of you."

I stood there, frozen in place. I was hearing what he was saying, but I couldn't make sense of it.

"Wait, hold up a minute. You're going to have to slow down." I put my hands to my head and sighed. "Okay, vapored-through me. What does that even mean?" Again the impossible was becoming my reality.

"And that night, in the water. When you thought you were stung by something," he continued.

I glared at him, not waiting for him to finish. "Can't you answer my first question, before you throw something else at me?" I yelled. I already knew something had happened that night. I knew I had been struck by something. My mind was whirling as I remembered the circular ball of light that I had seen under the water. The pain I had felt just before Ben pulled me to the surface. I knew the answer.

"It was her?" I said, making more of a statement than asking a question. I took a deep breath. "And now she's here for me. So she can finish whatever it was she started." My voice was getting louder, and I could feel my face getting hot. It felt like I was going to throw up. "What does she want with me?" I lowered my voice.

"Me…she wants you to lead her to me. She knows she can get to me through you." His answer was so simple, and yet it sent chills down my spine. I didn't need any more explanation; I knew what he meant.

"And what about Detective Baker? What if he finds you first?"

"He knows I'm here. We are trying to work together. I've told him as much about it as I can. They want to keep this quiet at all costs."

"So, when he was here this morning, he was just fishing to see what I knew or what I would tell him?" I was suddenly angry. I needed to be angry about something. "Trying to set me up." My face was beginning to feel hot again.

"It's okay, I think he really is trying to understand. They've agreed to let me try to stop her. They don't want the military getting involved. They are trying to keep the news media out of it. They are already asking too many questions? They know it's to everyone's advantage for me to be the one to take care of this." The concern in his voice scared me.

"They, who's they? The government? Do they know about everything? About you?" His silence told me that they did. "And by taking care of it, you mean taking care of her…Sariai. You'll have to do what? Get rid of her?"

"She has to be absorbed. She and her companion. Before she does any more harm to anyone or anything. Before they carry out her plan." He walked over and picked up the box again.

"Plan, you know about it? You know what she is planning?" I walked over to where he stood.

"I've already told you too much, the more you know, the more danger you're in." He set the box down and put his hands on my shoulders. "I can't let anything happen to you. I won't let it." He gently pulled me to his chest. I could feel his rapid heartbeat against my face.

"You are not going to lose me." The burning feeling of my anger began to melt away. "Maybe I can help you," I said softly. "You said yourself I may have some of her power. I have to show you something." I took his hand and began to lead him across the hardwood floor.

"I can't let you—"

"Shhh." I put my finger to my lips.

I quietly opened the bedroom door and looked out into the hallway. No one was in sight as I pulled him out of the room and across the hall.

"I can't let you do that, she's too powerful still," he finished his thought as I locked the bathroom door behind us.

"Well…Umm, maybe you can help me after all," he said teasingly and pulled me closer to him.

"Funny!" I rolled my eyes.

He smiled as I led him across the small room. I wanted him to see what was happening to my body. We stood in front of the sink. I turned on the faucet and put my hands under the stream of water. I looked at him, waiting for his reaction as they began to disappear into the water's flow. "I have one more question for you," I whispered. It only took a moment. Like all the times before, they faded into vapor—leaving the rest of my body perfectly intact. "Why?"

He said nothing. He gently put his hands on my waist, forcing me toward the tub. Facing each other, he reached around me and turned the water on.

"What are you doing?" I asked. He slowly inched me backward and took my hand. I didn't resist as we stepped into the tub. I could feel his breath on my neck as he reached around me and pulled the lever for the shower.

"It's okay," he whispered. "Trust me." He slid the glass door shut.

We moved together until we were entirely under the stream of water that was flowing from the rain shower head. I knew what was happening to my body. He moved closer to me, pressing his against mine so that we were both standing under the water's warm flow.

I could see and feel our bodies intertwining and changing. He reached for my hands and took them in his. Even though they were like a vapor, I could feel his fingers wrap around mine. We moved together, circling each other, never letting loose of our grip. Then, suddenly, he stopped.

We stood there looking at each other. He began to move even closer to me. I could feel the temperature in my body rising. My heart was fluttering so fast I couldn't breathe. It felt like I was underwater, struggling for air yet at the same time not needing it.

He raised my arms above my head. The water ran from the tips of our fingers down to our toes into the tub below. I could feel his breath on my face as our bodies seemed to melt into one. The intense feeling that was burning inside me made me dizzy.

He let go of my hands and took a step back. "Come to me," he said.

I took a step forward when at the same instant, he moved toward me. *Is this really happening?* I thought as I felt the most incredible sense of pleasure. It felt as if my heart stopped for a moment. A sense of complete joy filled my soul. A feeling of completeness. Replaced with emptiness as soon as it was over. I turned to face him, the water from the shower head still flowed over our spirit-like bodies. We had literally passed through each other.

"You can control it," he said as we spun slowly under the flow. "Concentrate."

"I've tried...I can't," I whispered.

"Yes, you can. You just have to believe that you can."

Reaching out, he cupped my hands in his and brought them to his lips. "You can do anything, as long as you have faith in your power." He reached around me and turned the water off.

Hearing him say it, I almost believed it.

We stood there, as our bodies began to take back their form. He stepped out of the tub, leaving me there.

"Your clothes are wet," he teased as he took two towels from the rack and handed one of them to me.

"If that was what you meant before when you said she 'vapored-through' me. I can tell you one thing for certain... that is not what happened with her at the airport. I have never felt anything like that before."

My head began to spin. I felt my knees weaken—then everything went black.

Chapter Ten

It was a loud noise that jolted me awake. I sat straight up in my bed. "Ben?" I looked around the empty room. *Had I been dreaming?* I wondered again. *No, it couldn't have been a dream, could it?* Of course, it was only a dream, just like all the other dreams of him that I had had since I awoke in the hospital that day, all those months ago.

I threw the covers off and sat there on the side of the bed—trying to decide if I wanted to go downstairs, or just lay back down and pull them over my head. *If only it were that easy,* I thought.

I heard it again. Someone was knocking on the front door. I shoved the covers aside and slid my feet onto the wide-planked wooden floor. I walked over to the window and pulled the sheer aside. It was still light outside, but... something didn't seem quite right.

Oh my goodness, I thought, sucking in a breath. *I had told Aunt Abby I would be right down. How long ago was that?* I glanced at the clock on the bedside table. It read

7:10 AM. It was morning. Hours had passed. I let the curtain fall back into place.

I heard them talking as I entered the kitchen. "There you are," Anna said. "You are coming with me to register for classes today, aren't you?"

Aunt Abby was sitting at the table, drinking her morning coffee. "Did I sleep all night? Why didn't you wake me?" I was angry, not at Aunt Abby…just angry.

"Luvy, you were so tired, I checked in on you and decided to just let you rest."

"No! You should have woken me. How am I ever going to know what is a reality, and what is just a dream?" I shouted. I knew full well time and place had nothing to do with it. And it was not Aunt Abby's fault.

"I'm sorry, Luvy. I never thought you would be upset." She got up from the table and walked over to where I was standing. "Look, Anna has come to pick you up to go with her to the school today." She put her arm around my shoulder. I instantly felt the tension leave my body.

"I'm the one that's sorry," I murmured.

"It's okay, you don't have to apologize," she whispered. "But you had better hurry if you intend to go." She looked from me to Anna, who was still standing there…waiting.

"I don't even have time to get ready? I don't need to go."

"I know you don't need to, but I want you to. You have time…if you hurry," Anna said as she stood there, smiling. "Please!"

Oh, why not? I thought. *It would give me another chance to talk to Liam.* "You can come up with me while I get dressed if you want." I turned to go back up the stairs.

"Sure," she responded with her usual perkiness. Too perky for this early in the morning. She followed me as we made our way into the bedroom. I closed the door behind us.

"I'll just be a minute," I walked across the bedroom and began to open drawers, picking out a pair of jeans and a T-shirt.

"Why are you changing? You look fine with what you have on."

I suddenly realized I was not in my pajamas. I was still wearing the same clothes I had on yesterday. The ones I had on in the shower. The shower with Ben. I ran my hand down the front of my top, it was not even damp. *It had been a dream.*

"I must have fallen asleep in these." I felt like a little kid lying to their parents. "Like I said, I don't have to go," I raised my voice at her. "If you don't want to wait, then go ahead and leave."

"No, it's okay…go ahead and change." She walked over and sat on the bed. I took off the clothes I had on and slipped a T-shirt over my head.

"What's this?" she asked.

"What's what?" I turned to see what she was talking about. She had opened the box—Ben's box.

"What do you think you are doing? You can't just snoop in my things." I walked across the room and grabbed the box from her. I cradled it to my chest and then gently set it down on the nightstand.

"I'm sorry, I didn't mean to…" She shamefully hung her head.

"You didn't mean to what? Obviously, you did, or you would not have picked it up." I glared at her. "You really do need to learn some boundaries, or you're going to have a lot of trouble making new friends." I slid my legs into the pair of jeans and pulled them over my hips.

"I need to put this back in it," she whispered. She was sitting there holding a piece of paper in her hand. "I'm sorry. You took it away before I could put it back."

I slowly took the paper from her hand and stood there, staring at it. I had been through each and every item that was in the box…over and over again. I had memorized the things, every detail in the box. This piece of folded paper was not one that I recognized.

"Where did you get this?" I asked her.

She gave me a puzzled look. "I told you, from the box."

I closed my eyes and felt the squared corners of the folded paper. The smoothness of its surface. I raised it to my face as I inhaled the scent of it. This was not something that had been there. Yet, its scent was familiar. It smelled like Ben. I stood there staring at the neatly folded piece of paper.

"Christi, are you okay?" she asked shyly.

I knew she was talking to me, but I was not hearing her. I gazed blankly at the piece of paper, turned and slowly walked to the window as I unfolded it. I read the words that were written on the inside.

Never doubt the power that is within you...I don't.

I suddenly realized that it had not been a dream. Ben had been there. Everything had happened, just as I remembered it. A sense of relief poured over me, knowing it had not been a dream. Then a sudden chill sent a shiver down my spine for the very same reason. I slowly folded the paper and tucked it into the front pocket of my jeans. Anna sat there silently. I put on my shoes and stood to walk out of the bedroom.

"Are you ready?" I asked, opening the door to the hallway.

"You really are a weird one." She walked past me out the door.

"You are a good one to talk," I snapped.

She turned to look at me. We stared at each other for a second, then we both burst out laughing. It felt good.

"My dad said we can use the truck, but you need to drive. I don't have my permit yet. If that's okay." She was still talking as we stepped from the staircase into the kitchen. "Is it okay, Ms. Collins?"

Aunt Abby was still sitting at the table. "Is what okay?" she asked.

"Can I drive Manny's truck to the school?" I answered before Anna could.

"Oh, I don't know. Maybe I should take you, or we can ask your mom or Tom. They're not here though, they had to leave early. Poppie had a doctor's appointment this morning. We can call them." She stood and walked over to the desk where our phones were charging.

"It really is fine, my dad said we could." Anna was pleading her case. "We need to get going, though, have to be there at nine."

"Please, Aunt Abby, Mom will say no. You know she will. She treats me like I'm still a baby. Besides, it is not all day. We'll be back by early afternoon. We'll be back before they will. Won't we, Anna?" Anna shook her head in agreement. I walked over and kissed Aunt Abby on the cheek. "I'll be careful, it's just to the school." I reached around her to grab my phone.

"Fine, but come right home afterward," she said. "Make sure you have your license. And wear your seatbelts. It does have seatbelts, doesn't it?" We smiled as we made our way to the front door.

"Oh, my license," I walked back to the desk and picked up the small bag that contained my ID. "What would I do without you?" I hugged her, then turned toward the kitchen door where Anna was still standing, waiting. "Love you," I said, looking back at her. I closed the big wooden door behind us.

I couldn't hear her, but I knew what her response was… *To the moon and back.*

"It does have seat belts, doesn't it?" I smiled jokingly at Anna as I opened the driver's side door of the pickup truck that was parked in front of the barn.

"Uh, yeah." She climbed into the passenger side and pulled the belt across her body, snapping it into place.

I pulled myself up into the seat and hooked the belt around me. The engine rattled to a start. I backed up just enough to make the turn and head down the driveway to the main road.

"Thank you for agreeing to come with me," she broke the silence. "I know you didn't really want to. I appreciate it. It means a lot."

"It's okay. I am actually a little curious about the people here. I think some of them will be interesting." I glanced over at her.

"Like Liam?" she smiled.

"I am not interested in Liam, not in that way," I assured her.

"Do you have a boyfriend? Back home, I mean."

There was a long pause before I managed to answer. "I've dated a couple of guys. Never anyone special, until last spring." I paused, turning on the main road heading toward town.

"So there is a boyfriend."

"I'm not sure I would call him my boyfriend, but there is someone."

"What's his name? Tell me about him. What's he like?" She was rattling off questions before I could respond. "Was it him, the note I mean. Was it from him?"

"It's a long story." I could feel my face begin to turn red from the emotion that was welling up inside me.

"You don't need to answer. I can see it. You love him, don't you?" She reached across the seat and touched my arm.

A tear spilled onto my cheek. It felt like for the first time, I was letting myself feel what my heart was telling me. The deep emotions that just thinking of him brought out of me, the tingling sensation that ran through my body when I thought of him touching me. His lips pressing against mine. I was in love with Ben.

I wiped the tears from my cheeks as the school came into view. The parking lot was already full of cars, students were beginning to make their way into the building.

"Look, there he is," she said excitedly. She rolled down the window of the truck and yelled. "Hey, Liam." He stopped and looked at us as I pulled into one of the few open parking spaces. "God, he's cute," she sighed, breathing her words. Staring at him, her face turned five shades of red.

"Remember, it's the cute ones you need to look out for." I slid out of the truck and closed the creaky door.

A small group of girls had already surrounded him. I could hear their flirty giggles as they shifted their hips and flipped their hair. All of them vying for his attention. Hoping they would be the one he would notice. His good looks and charm were infectious. And, it appeared they had all caught it.

The five of them turned to look in our direction. His attention was focused on us as we walked around the truck and onto the sidewalk.

"You are drooling again," I whispered to Anna as we approached the group.

"Hey, Anna, I see your friend decided to come after all," he chirped.

"Yes, I'm hoping that after today, she'll decide to stay for the school year," Anna said excitedly, stopping beside them.

"That is not going to happen," I quickly inserted and moved to stand beside her.

"You think you're too good or what?" one of the girls said sharply.

"Yeah, who is she, anyway?" Another of the four spewed, wanting to make her presence known.

"This is Christi, she's my neighbor," Liam answered. "Or at least for a couple of weeks she is," he smiled, correcting himself.

"You do not have to speak for me. I am a big girl." I stopped beside them.

"Is she illegal too?" the same girl, the blonde one, spewed. They all giggled as if she had said something funny.

"Do you have a problem or something?" I glared at her.

"Do you?" she glared back.

"Let's just go in." Anna pulled on my arm.

"They're just kidding," Liam tried to cover for them.

"Yeah, we're harmless," one of the others chimed in.

"Christi," Anna pleaded. "Please, let's just go."

They huddled together snickering. Liam just stood there, looking at us.

Anna was right, you are not worth our time, I thought as we walked toward the entrance of the building without looking back at them.

"That's how they are," Anna said. The glass double doors closed behind us. "I just try to ignore them."

"Anna, you cannot just ignore that. You have to take up for yourself. Besides, what are they talking about? Illegal? Are you and your dad not US citizens?" I whispered as we approached the registration tables. Tears were welling up in her eyes. "Anna..." I touched her arm.

"Why does it matter to them?" She stopped there in the hallway. "I'm still a person with feelings. I've always tried to treat people the way I want to be treated." Her tone was childlike as she looked down at the floor. Tears spilled down her face. "No matter how they treat me. Isn't that what we're supposed to do?" Her sincerity was so innocent.

"Yes, but you cannot let yourself be bullied by those bit—" I stopped myself before the words came out of my mouth. After all, saying it would have been just like them. I reached out and touched her shoulder. "You're a better person than any of us, Anna. We can all learn from you."

She smiled. The entrance door of the school opened, and the chatter of students filled the hallway, echoing off the concrete walls. A flood of students passed by us, filling the lines at the registration tables. We took our place, waiting for our turn for Anna to get her paperwork.

I spent the next few hours following Anna, going from room to room, meeting with teachers, hearing goals and objectives for the upcoming year. Time after time having to repeat, "I am just a visitor, and I am not enrolling for my senior year."

We were given instructions that, upon completion of the orientation, we were to head to the cafeteria, where snacks would be served and to receive schedules. Anna stopped as we approached the doors that lead inside the cafeteria.

"I've got what I need, let's just go on home," she said abruptly.

I could see the reason for her sudden disinterest. There they were, the same group of girls. Standing just inside the doorway, handing out the schedules.

"Anna, you need to get your schedule. You have been waiting for this. You made me come for crying out loud!" She looked toward the front entrance and then back to me.

"You are going to get your schedule. Don't let them ruin this for you." I was stern with her.

She turned and reluctantly followed me as we took our place in the line that was beginning to form at the door's entrance.

"Okay, what's your name again?" the blonde asked, looking at Anna as we stepped up in the line. "Anna something?" She tapped her finger on the side of her chin as her sidekicks snickered. "Anna what? Anna Hispania?" All four of them laughed.

"Look, you! I have had just about enough. Are you threatened by Anna or something? Are you really that insecure?" I wanted her to know that I could see her motives. "Anna is three times the person than any of you are. She deserves to be treated with respect. And you three, do any of you have a freaking mind of your own? Or do you just go along with whatever she says or does? Let me tell you… that will get you nowhere fast. You should take a lesson from her"—I nodded to Anna—"on how you should treat people and show them a little respect. Oh, but none of you can even spell it, can you? Let alone practice it. Be glad that I am not going to school here," I hissed at them. "You all need a reality check." Everyone got quiet.

"Anna Ramirez," Anna murmured.

"Oh, yes, here you are. All…the…way…in the back," she drew out her words as she pulled the sheet from the clipboard and handed it to Anna.

Anna shyly took the paper from her. "Thank you," she whispered. I followed her, glaring back at them as we walked into the cafeteria and found an empty table.

"How did your morning go?" It was from Liam. He came in and sat down at our table across from us. "Do we have any classes together?" He took Anna's schedule that was lying on the table in front of her and began to compare the two. "We do, it looks like we have a couple together." He slid the paper back across the surface. Anna didn't say anything as I sat there looking at him knowing that he was pretending to be someone he wasn't.

"Do they offer an anti-bullying class? Maybe your uncle the detective could teach it. And you and your friends should sign up for it," I spewed at him. Anna elbowed me in the side. It wasn't going to stop me. "Maybe he would be interested in a lot of your activities." I wanted him to know that I knew something, but I also wanted him to wonder just how much.

His expression did not change, he just sat there staring at me. "I have that bonfire party at the waterfall tonight. You two are coming, right?" He was talking to both of us, but he never took his eyes off me. As if he knew what I was thinking. *Of course, he did.*

"Yes, I'm excited about coming. We're excited, aren't we, Christi?" Anna perked up, smiling at him.

"Why would they be invited?" It was her again, the blonde. She slid onto the seat beside Liam and put her arm around him. The other girls had followed her and took their places beside her like little minions. "We just can't wait to get to know each other a little better, can we?" Her sarcastic tone turned my stomach. "Why don't we start now? What was your name again, anyway?" she asked. Twisting her lip to the side and squinting her eyes, she looked at me.

"It is Christi. And why would we not be invited?" I welcomed the confrontation with her. "Unless Liam here only does what you tell him to. Is that how it is Liam? You like your girlfriends, telling you what to do?" He still had not taken his eyes off me.

The voice of the principal came over the loudspeaker. Citing excitement and expectations for the upcoming year.

She stared at me across the table. "Do you know you talk weird? All high and mighty. Do you really think you are better than us? Where are you from, anyway?"

"Maybe she's a princess," Liam said. A chill ran down my body. Frozen, I recalled the words...*the girl Ion calls princess*...words that I had heard that night in the ocean.

"What?" I asked, my voice suddenly shaking.

He looked at me, smirking. "I was referring to your bracelet. That's what it says, doesn't it?"

I felt my wrist and covered the chain with my hand as if I was protecting it.

She glanced toward Anna. "Are you one of those so-called *Dreamers*, like her?" She raised her hands, making air-quotes as she spoke. They huddled together and snickered like little kids. "Do you even realize that you talk like that? My guess is that you...*do not*." Again she made air quotes, mocking me.

"Do you realize that you are a *bitch,* my guess is that you...*do not?*" I used some air quotes of my own. I could feel my face turning red from the anger that was building inside me. Anna touched my arm. I so wanted to keep giving her a piece of my mind.

"Girls!" The voice was stern. One of the teachers who had been sitting at the table next to us was now standing

124

over us. "Is there a problem?" she asked, looking at each of us.

"No, no problem at all," Liam said as he shifted uneasily in his seat.

"Then show the principal some respect," she instructed. Then she slowly returned to her seat. Occasionally glancing our direction throughout the rest of the speech.

"See you tonight, Liam," Anna said as we were dismissed. She quickly got up and headed for the door. My conversation with them was over, at least for now.

"Come tonight, around eight," Liam said as I turned to leave. "Everyone who is anyone will be there."

"Of course! I'll be there," the blonde said, still hanging on to him.

I could not resist. I had no doubt that he was who I thought he was. I turned back to where they all were still sitting.

"Will Sariai be there?" I asked.

"Sariai, who's that?" the blonde asked, turning to look at him. Her puzzled look pleased me.

"I wouldn't miss it," I said under my breath as I walked away.

Chapter Eleven

The ride back to the ranch was quiet. Just occasional small talk about some of the comments from the teachers concerning the upcoming semester.

"I'm not so sure we should go tonight." There was a sadness in her voice.

"Don't you want to?" I was surprised. She turned to look out the window without answering.

"I think we should, Anna, you can't avoid them. I'll be there with you. Besides, you know how much you like to look at Liam." I tried to lighten her mood.

"He likes you more than me," she said, her eyes fixed on the window.

"What? No, believe me. If Liam is interested in me, it is not in the way you think."

She turned back to look at me. "What other way is there?"

"Just trust me on this one. But you're right to be cautious about his motives. There is more to him than you know, more than any of us knows."

"What does that mean?" Her frown made her nose wrinkle. "Why do you have to be so mysterious?" Then, just like that, her mood lightened. "Ooh, I know. Maybe he's a werewolf," she laughed. "Like in those movies. Yes, that's it." She straightened herself in the seat beside me. "The wolf, maybe it was Liam. And you saved him, that's why he likes you, he can't control it, he's drawn to you." Her tone was dramatic as she rolled her eyes.

"Wow, you have it all figured out—we are busted!" I threw my hands up in the air. We laughed.

I slowed the truck, making the turn onto the drive that led to the farmhouse. Its metal frame squeaked as it dropped from the blacktop road to the gravel drive.

"How did you do that anyway?" she asked. "I know I said we didn't have to talk about it, but I can't just forget that it happened."

We pulled to a stop in front of the barn. "How did I do what?" Knowing exactly what she was referring to.

"The wolf, his leg, you touched it, and it healed somehow. Like the cut from the trap was not even there. How did you do that?"

"I don't think you remember it like it really was. You were just excited, and a little bit of blood can look like a lot." I tried to sound convincing.

"No, I know what I saw!" She shook her head, sounding like me now. I remember how Ben had tried to convince me that I had not seen what I knew that I had. She deserved the truth too.

I understood her confusion…I didn't even understand it. "I'm not sure what I did or didn't do. Honestly, Anna, it's the not knowing that scares me the most."

"You know it's a gift," she said softly, reaching over and touching my hands. They were shaking. "It's okay," she whispered. "Thank you for being there with me today…for taking up for me with those girls. You're right, I do need to stand up to them. But not till after the party at the water-fall tonight." She unbuckled her seatbelt and opened the creaky door. "I just want to fit in and have fun just once."

"Anna, you do not have anything to prove to those girls, or to anyone else for that matter." Sitting there, she seemed so sad and childlike. I unbuckled my belt, opened the driver's side door, and slid out of the truck. She slid off the seat, closed the creaky door, and came around the front and stood there looking out past the barn toward the mountain trail that leads to the waterfall.

"We are going tonight, right? Anna…right?"

"There's my girl. I thought I was going to have to take one of the horses out," her dad said, coming out of the barn. He sat down what looked to be a toolbox and walked over to the wooden fence that surrounded the barn lot.

Anna ran over, stepped up onto the first rung of the fence, and hugged him. It made me think of my dad. I had not talked to him since we had arrived at the airport. *I'll call him this afternoon,* I thought, watching the closeness between them.

"I'm heading out to work on some fencing. Want to come with me?" he asked her.

"Sure!" she answered excitedly.

"Miss Christi, do you want to come along?" he asked as Anna jumped down from the fence.

"No. I had better check on how Poppie's doing. And I need to call my dad." I walked toward the house.

"What time are we going tonight?" she called out.

I suddenly wished I had not pushed her about going tonight. What if I had seen something in the water? Everyone there would be in danger.

"Let me check with Aunt Abby, I'll let you know. Maybe we can meet around eight." I started up the steps to the porch.

"What's this? You have plans?" She had piqued her dad's interest.

"Just a party with some of my new friends from school." I heard her say as they climbed into the pickup and the doors shut. "See you later," she yelled to me, waving as she hung out of the window. They pulled around the barn and headed down the path to the outer pasture.

Friends? I thought. I waved to them as the front door opened, and Aunt Abby stepped out onto the porch.

"I thought I heard the truck. How did it go?" she asked. She moved over to the porch swing and patted the empty space beside her. I walked over and sat down on the green-and-white striped padded cushion that made the wooden swing a little more comfortable.

"Anna got her schedule...she's excited, I guess." I looked out toward the outer pasture, the truck was no longer in sight. "Some girls are bullying her, though."

"Oh no, she is such a sweet girl. I hate to hear that." Aunt Abby's tone reflected her concern. "Has she talked to the principal about it? Does her dad know?"

"I tried to get her to take up for herself. I tried to take up for her. She just chooses to ignore it. She thinks if she treats them nice, then they will be nice to her. That is not going to happen with those four, I can tell you that. I've seen it at my school. If you don't put them in their place, it will only get worse." I remembered some of the kids at my school who were bullied. Most of them were quiet and would sit by themselves at lunch. They just didn't seem to fit in. They were teased and harassed. Other students would talk about them behind their backs. Now, I wished I would have done more to stand up for them.

"She has the right idea, Luvy. Unfortunately, some people just seem to enjoy hurting others. Most of the time, it's because they are unhappy themselves. The sad part is, we don't have any idea what they have gone through to cause them to act that way."

"That's no excuse, Aunt Abby."

"I know," she whispered. "Maybe you can help encourage her to be strong, but still be kind." Aunt Abby always tried to see the bright side of things. That's what I loved most about her. But she was wrong this time.

"With these girls, I'm not sure that's possible." I shifted in the swing as I gently pushed against the floor. We began to sway back and forth. "We are invited to a party at Liam's tonight, maybe that will give her a chance to fit in a little bit." I saw the opportunity to let those plans be known. I did want to go to the waterfall, but not to make friends. I was afraid of what might happen there. Of what might happen if I didn't go and more importantly...what might happen if I did.

"Party? That sounds like fun. Will be good for both of you. Maybe we should just hang out here this afternoon then."

"Where is everyone?" I suddenly realized that my mom's car was still gone.

"I don't want you to worry, he's okay. But they had to take Poppie on to the VA hospital. Something about his heartbeat being out of rhythm. She thought they might keep him overnight. If they do, they plan to stay over too, instead of coming home and then having to drive back in the morning." Her voice stayed calm as she explained.

"Wow, I hope it's nothing serious."

"Me too, Luvy, me too." I leaned over and laid my head on her shoulder. "So…it's just us for the rest of the day, what do you want to do?" She rubbed her hand along the side of my face.

"Well, the party is not until tonight." I sat up in the swing. "We have plenty of time, though. We can even do something now if you want. I just need to call my dad first."

I took my phone out of my back pocket. No answer; all I got was his voice mail. "Hey, Dad, just checking in. Everything is good. I miss you. Talk to you later. Love you."

I sat there holding the phone thinking about how I had been keeping everything that was happening to me from my dad. I was keeping it from everyone. As different as Anna and I were. We did have some things in common. *Just like her being bullied*, I thought, *no one could help me either. We both had some things we would have to deal with on our own.*

"How about we go up to the lake and hike your favorite trail?" Aunt Abby stopped the swing and looked at me.

"Yeah, that sounds great. I just need to change my shoes," I stood and walked toward the door.

"I just need to change my shoes too," she said, smiling. "So I'll meet you back right here."

I smiled in agreement. She put her arm around me as we went inside and made our way up the stairs. I stepped into the bedroom as she continued on down the hall to her room.

"I'll only be a minute," she called back to me.

I pulled the hiking shoes that I had packed for the trip from my bag. I thought of how Poppie and I had always loved to walk the trails by the lake as I sat down on the side of the bed to put them on.

The paper crackled as I bent over. I took the note from my front pocket and reread it, tracing the words with my fingers. The words of encouragement should have made me feel better…but it was that power within me, the meaning of the words that were written there, that was also scaring me to death.

Because of it, had I hurt Poppie in some way? I thought of his reaction when I had touched him. *If I had the power to heal with a touch, did I have the ability to hurt someone?* How could I put those thoughts away and enjoy the afternoon with Aunt Abby? I would have to try.

We drove to the trailhead, talking about all the times we had hiked this trail. The three-mile trek would wind up the mountainside, around the east side of the lake, past the dam at the power plant, then back down, ending up on the path where we started.

"Not too many hikers today," she observed.

There was only one other car parked in the big gravel lot. She pulled in beside it. We walked around the back of the car and started across the lot to the trailhead.

"Isn't that the detective's car?" I asked, staring at the government plates.

"Yes, I think it is." She was already walking toward the trail, seeming to not be giving it another thought.

Why would he be here? I wondered. It kept rolling over and over in my head as we walked along. We never talked much when we hiked. Only an occasional comment about a bird or a wildflower that we saw along the trail. Taking a moment here and there to absorb the beauty of nature that was all around us. We talked about Poppie and shared memories. But mostly we laughed and just enjoyed being together, stopping to rest for just a couple of minutes when we reached the top of the trail.

The sound of the water spilling over the dam filled the air as we walked along the side of the lake. I could barely make out the massive concrete structure ahead as I looked through the limbs and branches of the trees that overhung the trail along the bank. There were flashes of light from the sun's rays as it reflected off the metal walkway that ran the width of the dam over to the power plant. A new hydro-power plant had been built down by the river. This old plant had not yet been torn down. It was left vacant, still standing across the lake as a reminder of the days gone by. Its massive distinctive structure was like a ghost from the past that loomed over the lake. "DANGER KEEP OUT" signs were posted along the fencing that surrounded the property. You could see them from the opposite side of the lake, with their symbols and large red and black lettering: A Nuclear Power Plant.

"Didn't Poppie used to work there?" I asked, breaking the silence.

"Yes, he actually retired from there. Tom has always thought that his working there contributed to his health problems." She stopped just in front of me. We looked across at the sprawling site with its odd-shaped stacks and buildings of what used to be the only power source for the whole valley.

We were making our way along the wooded trail. "Why haven't they taken it down?"

"I think they decided it was more dangerous to tear it down than to just leave it alone." She stopped and put her hands on her hips as she answered.

The dam was in full view now. We could hear the roar of the water as it flowed over the spillway. The water was so beautifully still as it rushed into the structure. It seemed so peaceful until it began to churn into white foam as it was pulled through the grates and down the opposite side of the concrete dam.

"Let's get a picture," I said, reaching for my phone. Squeezing our faces together, we smiled for the selfie with the lake as our backdrop.

"Here, let me get one of you." She took my phone and walked a couple of feet away. I made different poses, making goofy faces as we laughed. "Okay, that's a good one," she said.

"Let me see! Let me see!" I hurried over as we huddled together, shading the screen as we scrolled through the photos.

"Wait, what is that?" I tapped the screen a few times as it magnified the images on the screen. "There! Is that someone?" I whirled around, looking at the spot that was captured in the photo.

"It looks like a person standing on the walkway." She looked at the walkway and back to the image. There was no sign of anyone. We stood there for a moment. "I don't know, maybe it was a shadow or something. Those phone cameras can do some weird things," she said, then began to walk on down the trail. "Or I'm sure they have security that keeps an eye on things, to keep trespassers out. It could have been that."

I looked at the photo again. *Yes*, it was a person, but not a security guard. I recognized the silhouette on the screen—distorted image and all—I knew who it was. It was the man I had seen on the beach that night. The same man that was at the house this morning, looking for those two missing people.

"I think it was that detective. That must have been his car that we saw in the parking lot." I said.

"Yes, it must have been him. I'm sure he is still in the area looking for those missing kids. Are you coming, or can't you keep up with me?" Aunt Abby smiled back at me.

My heart sank as I thought of their families. He was not going to find them. At least not the people they were. And, he was asking about Ben. All the thoughts of why he was here and what it meant, ran a chill through me.

"I'm coming." I looked again at the walkway… Nothing.

I tried not to show the concern that was building in me. My insides were churning as I imagined the possibilities of why he was there. Was he looking there for the missing people? And if they had been there, then it meant that Sarai knew about the abandoned power plant. A nuclear power plant. I knew that if Ben was worried about her, then who knows what she was capable of. She would have to know her time was running out. She would make herself known soon. I decided right then, if it was me she wanted, then it was me she would get. Before she did something or anyone else got hurt. Just like Ben had said.

I followed Aunt Abby as we wound down the back side of the narrow loop that would lead us back to the trailhead. I quickly glanced at my phone. The time on the screen read three o'clock.

We both heard the snap of the dry limb at the same time. We turned around to see him standing there in the path we had just walked. It was Detective Baker.

"Ladies, beautiful day for a hike," he said as he approached us.

"Yes, sir, it is," Aunt Abby said. "Christi thought that it might have been you that we saw on the walkway at the dam."

"You should not sneak up on people," I snapped at him and quickly turned away. I could feel my body begin to shake.

"I'm sorry if I startled you." He had stopped just a couple of feet from us, holding out his hand to Aunt Abby.

"Any news about those kids?" She shook his hand.

"No, not yet. But we are still looking. If they're out here, I'll find them."

"You think they might be in the old power plant?" she continued to question him. I held my hands behind my back, trying to control my trembling.

"We are just checking out every possibility. There is a fallout shelter underneath the old plant. It leads to an underwater tunnel into one of the caves down the way." His weight shifted as he explained. "We'll have to get some divers in there. If they want to hide, it would be a good place."

Suddenly his stature changed, his body tensed, his hand reached inside his jacket and, just like that, was pointing a gun in our direction.

"Don't move," he calmly stated.

It was then that I heard it, a low moan—no...it was more of a growl. I recognized it. I began to slowly turn in the direction of the sound.

"Don't move," he repeated.

There were two of them, about ten yards away from us. Teeth snarling, they stood there, staring at us as if they would attack at any second.

"Now, try not to panic—don't turn around, but walk very slowly toward me," he very calmly stated.

Aunt Abby began to slowly back toward him.

"Stop! Don't shoot," I yelled, throwing my arms out... as if I could stop a bullet if he decided to shoot.

"Luvy!" Aunt Abby yelled, reaching for me.

I stood there looking at the wolves that were now facing me—standing their ground.

"Okay, listen to me. I'm going to shoot in the air, just to scare them away. When I do, I want you to run this way and get behind me." His tone was still calm, yet firm.

"Luvy, do what he says!" Panic and fear riddled her voice.

"Stop!" I yelled again. Suddenly, there was movement behind the two beautiful animals that stood in front of me.

Their thick fur bristled and seemed to stand on end. Their magnificent eyes never shifted from me. There was movement from behind them, another one, walking slowly toward us. It was bigger. It made its way through the tall grass that swayed in the light breeze. It was the same wolf that Anna and I had freed the day before.

At that moment, it was as if we were all frozen in time. My eyes seemed to be out of focus. Everything around me seemed to stop. Everything…except the huge red and gray wolf that had moved around the other two and was slowly walking toward me.

I turned my head to look at Aunt Abby and the detective. They were just standing there, Aunt Abby's arms outstretched, reaching out to me. Detective Baker was looking in my direction with his gun, still pointing in the air. It was like they were in a trance of some kind.

The beautiful animal was so much bigger than he had seemed just the day before. *It's ok, no one is going to hurt you.* I don't know whether I whispered the words out loud, or if it was only in my mind.

He was so close now that I could feel his hot breath on my legs as he sniffed my scent, all the while…circling me. I could hear the leaves and twigs crackling underneath his weight. I stood still. His body was so close I felt his fur against my calf as he moved around me and stood a few feet away, facing me. He sniffed the air, pawed the ground and then suddenly—a shot rang out.

Everything came back into focus. All three turned and ran into the thick brush.

My heart was pounding. I finally took a breath.

Chapter Twelve

"What were you thinking, Luvy?" Aunt Abby came from behind me, wrapped her arms around me, and hugged me tightly. I just stood there, still looking in the direction the wolves had run.

"I'm glad I came across you guys when I did. Thankful that the shot scared them away." Detective Baker put his handgun back inside his jacket. "You need to be very careful when you are out on the trails, wolves are not the only dangers out here," he said.

"Yes, we always are. You just don't ever expect to see wolves this close to the trails," Aunt Abby responded.

"Stay aware of your surroundings at all times," he said, looking around us for any sign that they might still be close. "The packs may be getting more aggressive, so they could come closer to the main roads and to people. I'll be sure to make the Game Wardens aware of it as soon as I get back." He walked ahead of us on the trail. "I'll walk back the rest of the way with you, just in case."

We fell in behind him, winding around the path. His eyes were fixed on the trees and undergrowth alongside the pathway. It didn't take us long before we were back at the trail entrance. The lot was filled with cars.

"Looks like there may be other hikers on the trail, I'd better go check things out. Those wolves are still out there. Be careful, ladies, keep an eye out," he warned.

"Thank you, and you be careful too," Aunt Abby called back to him, as we walked across to our car.

We sat there for a moment in the car. Catching our breath, thinking about what had happened.

"Wow, it was a good thing that he came upon us when he did. If he hadn't scared them away." Her body shivered a little as she started the car. "I don't even want to think about it," she sighed, her voice quivered with emotion.

"How close did they get to us, Aunt Abby?"

"You saw them, Luvy, they were about ten yards or so away. Too close." She leaned over and kissed my cheek. "I'm so glad you're safe."

"The big one…the red and grey one, did you see him?" I pushed for more.

"Yes. Oh my goodness, so thankful Detective Baker was able to get a shot off before it got any closer." She backed the car out of the parking space. "God was watching over us today, that's for sure."

Again, I couldn't make sense of it. It seemed as though neither of them had seen everything that had happened. Or, if they did…somehow, they didn't remember it. I just knew that it did happen, that somehow time and space had stood still.

"Do you want to grab something to snack on while we're out? We could even make an early dinner since it's just us," she asked, pulling out of the parking area onto the main road.

"I don't think so, I'm not even hungry. Besides, I would like to take Midnight out for a ride this afternoon." I intended to go back to the waterfall. The answers I needed were there. Sariai was there, I was sure of it.

"Oh, Luvy, I don't want you going out. Especially by yourself, not after what we just went through. Seeing those wolves, so close to the trail. Tom said he's been hearing them at night. They could be and probably are what has killed some of the cattle. I don't want you going out, especially after dark." She was emphatic.

"Oh, I don't plan on going alone. And we'll be back before dark. Anna and I are invited to a party tonight. It's at Liam Baker's, at the waterfall on their property. I just thought we could ride before we have to get ready for the party. Besides...I promised Anna that we would go for a ride," I lied.

I had not talked to Anna about taking the horses out. It was becoming a habit of lying to Aunt Abby. Hopefully, someday, I could be honest with her and tell her everything, but...not yet.

"No, I don't think so. You heard what Detective Baker said," she said, shaking her head.

"Are we just supposed to stay inside all the time, not go out because there may be a wolf? We are in Wyoming, we are in the mountains, Aunt Abby, duh! Of course, there are wolves," I whined. "They ran away, didn't they? Besides, the farm is several miles from here, please, Aunt Abby." I was trying to convince her there was nothing to worry about, knowing full well the danger that was there were not wolves.

"Luvy, I did see them, that's the problem. This time we were lucky that Detective Baker was there. But what about next time? That's what I'm afraid of."

She was not going to budge. I sighed in disgust and laid my head back against the seat.

I opened my eyes as we were turning onto the driveway leading to the farmhouse. Sitting up in my seat, I brushed my hair back away from my face.

Aunt Abby glanced over at me as she spoke. "I know you are responsible. It's not that at all. It sounds like Anna really needs someone to talk to. You are a good friend to her, and I think that you both need a friend to talk to right now." I just sat there as she pulled to a stop in front of the house. "So, I'll give in. But…you need to eat something before you think about riding, and you have to be back before it starts to get dark." She reached over and tucked a strand of hair behind my ear. "Are you okay?" she asked. "Or are you just in shock that I changed my mind?" She smiled, winking at me. "You know, I could go too. Poppie does have more than two horses."

"I know, and of course, that would be awesome," I responded excitedly, trying to sound enthusiastic. "But I really want to talk to Anna, girl bonding time," I inserted, forcing a smile.

"I understand," she said softly, patting my arm.

"Thank you, I love you, Aunt Abby." I leaned over and kissed her cheek.

"To the moon and back." She opened the car door and stepped out onto the gravel driveway.

"Hey, you two." It was Anna, coming from the barn lot.

"Back at you, sweetie." Aunt Abby waited for her to come around the front of the car and gave her a hug. "Christi tells me you guys have some plans this evening."

"Yes, ma'am, I am looking forward to the party at Liam's tonight," she blushed a little as she spoke. "I'm just waiting for my dad. We're going to run into town, to get me a new bathing suit, but he said we could use the truck again to go to Liam's."

"I thought you guys were taking the horses out before the party?" Aunt Abby looked at me, her forehead wrinkled, reflecting her confusion. "Sounds like maybe you had better postpone your ride."

"No, we can't!" I was emphatic. "We have to go now… like we planned." I insisted, glaring at her. "Anna? Right?"

"We planned to take the horses out now?" Anna asked, curling her lip.

"That's right, remember, we are taking the horses out for a ride before the party." I inserted quickly.

"We can do that…I guess. Just like we planned." She rolled her eyes, nervously shifting her weight from side to side.

"We'll be back in plenty of time to get ready for the party. I'll be right back," I said, turning toward the house. "Besides. Why do you need a bathing suit? You are not getting back in that waterfall, remember, you promised."

"Waterfall!" Aunt Abby said excitedly. "I'll have to check that out sometime this week."

"Don't get in, she'll freak out. And I do still need a suit."

I faintly heard her as I ran up the front steps and through the front door, the screen door snapping shut behind me. Stuffing a couple of protein bars in my pocket, I grabbed two bottles of water from the refrigerator, then headed back outside.

"You haven't eaten," Aunt Abby began to protest as I walked past her toward the barn.

I held up one of the protein bars as I slid open the big wooden door of the barn. She reminded us again to be careful. I reassured her we would be, and that we would be back in time to get ready for the party.

"Besides, you always worry too much. What would you do if I did move out here? Worry all the time?" I smiled back at her as I pulled Anna into the barn.

"Okay, you know I am all for taking the horses out. But what was all that about?" Anna asked when we were out of hearing distance, safely inside the barn.

"Listen, here is what we are going to do." I glanced out the open door toward the house, Aunt Abby was sitting on the porch swing. "You are going to ride with me to the gate at the outer pasture. Then you are coming back without Aunt Abby seeing you." I began to saddle Midnight, putting the bottles of water into a bag that hung on one side.

"And why are we doing this?" She frowned as she grabbed another saddle. "Are you meeting someone?"

I ignored her questions, turned, and began to lead Midnight out of the barn. She followed right behind me, leading Summer.

"Ms. Abby, would you tell my dad that I forgot to tell him about our plans," Anna called out as we passed by the porch.

"I will." Aunt Abby nodded and waved to us as we continued around the side of the barn. "Don't go too far. Be careful," she yelled.

Anna waited until we were through the gate before she questioned me again. "Why aren't you coming back with me, and why do I have to sneak back?"

I didn't answer or even look at her as I closed the gate behind us. We headed toward the outer fence. That would be as far as she would go, that was all there was to it.

It never gets old, I thought as we rode through the meadow. The beauty of the mountains, standing against the brilliant blue sky. Its beauty was breathtaking. I didn't know what I thought I would find at the waterfall, or what I would do if I did. I just knew I could not sit back and wait for Ben to show me or to tell me what to do. I had to find out for myself. This was something I had to do for me.

I pulled open the large gate that surrounded the perimeter of the outer fields. "This is as far as you go," I said to her.

"Nope, I'm going with you." She nudged her horse forward through the open gate.

"Oh, no, you're not! Go home, Anna! I'll see you at the party later." I tried to sound as normal as possible.

"What's going on, Christi? Are you meeting Liam?"

"No, don't be stupid," I yelled at her, disgustingly. "I am getting really tired of this jealousy thing with you! I am not interested in Liam...not in that way!" I grabbed hold of Summer's reins.

"You keep saying that, but what other way is there?" We glared at each other. "Okay, if I go back, I go straight to your aunt and let her know that you lied and that you are up to something."

"Why are you so damn irritating to me and won't say a peep to those bitches at your school?" I was irritated with her.

"Because I'm worried about you. If it's not Liam... then what?"

I paused for a moment before I looked up at her. "I can't tell you, and I don't have time to explain it to you. I am not going to let you get involved."

"You can't, or you won't?"

"What if I can't protect you?" I whispered. "What if I can't even protect myself?"

"Okay, now you are really freaking me out," she said, her voice shaking. "That's all the more reason for me to either go with you or go to your family about it. I'm not going to just let you ride off into God knows what...and me to just go back and pretend as if nothing is happening. Surely you can see that I can't do that?"

"I told you, I can't let you get involved."

"What are you talking about? I'm already involved. If it's something that dangerous, then we need to let the authorities know."

"No!" I yelled at her.

"Then, I can't let you go alone."

She was not going to give in. We stood there, staring at each other. Time was wasting.

"Then you do what I say, and I don't want to hear another word out of you," I dropped the reins and closed the gate behind her.

We made our way around the same mountain path that we had just two days ago. There were so many thoughts racing through my mind. *What if she was there? Sariai... and what was I going to do if she was?* She was near...I could feel it. She would need to be near water, I was sure of that. For some reason, deep down, I knew she would be at the waterfall. I couldn't wait for her to make the first move. If she were here for me, then she would come for me. I had to make sure it was on my time and on my terms. And the time was now. All I could do was pray Ben would be there too. I stopped at the same spot I had two nights earlier.

"We need to walk from here," I told her as I dismounted Midnight and tied his reins onto a branch of a tree that was alongside the path.

The stillness that surrounded us made me pause for a moment. Looking around, I noticed the daisy-looking flowers that were growing at its base. They were just like the ones in the bouquet that my mom had placed in my bedroom. Its beautiful yellow petals with dark black centers.

"They're called chocolate flowers," Anna said. "They bloom all summer."

Taking it between my fingers, I leaned down, breathing in the scent of it. It allowed me to think of something else, even if it was just for a moment. Long enough to think about how awesome God is to have created such majesty in the mountain ranges, and yet placed such intricate details in the petal of a flower. His handy work was all around us. The same God who allowed both good and evil to exist. I was not wise enough to know why. I just knew He would be with me to see me through. Faith was all I needed. I whispered a prayer to myself.

We crept along the path. Both of us felt the weight of not knowing what we might encounter when we got to the waterfall.

I motioned to Anna to get down low. We began to creep along as we neared the waterfall. Kneeling, we peered through the thick weeds that grew along the path to see if anyone was nearby. There was no one.

"Anna, this is what I need you to do." We began to move toward the falls. "The ledge behind the waterfall. I want you to get in behind there and stay there until I get back."

"Where are you going? And why on earth do I need to hide?"

"I'm getting in." I began to take off my clothes. "There is an underwater cave. I think that girl, the one that's missing, what was her name? Audrey, I think she might be in there."

"Who? What are you talking about?"

I did not respond, as I laid my clothes along the side of the pool of water.

"Why would you think that?" Her questioning tone was louder now. We stood there silently by the side of the pool of water. "Then I'm getting in with you." She started to pull her top over her head.

"No!" I grabbed her arm.

"What if you're right?" She was trying to reason with me. "What if she's hurt and you need my help?" she asked again.

I put my hands on her shoulders. "Listen to me, if something goes wrong and I'm not back…then I need you here…to go get help."

"Oh, so then you want me to go get help when it's too late." Her voice was shaky, her body trembling.

"Anna, listen to me carefully. I can hold my breath a really long time. I have done it before, just the other night." Her eyes looked from me to the water. "It'll be okay. What I'm telling you is if I'm not back…go for help."

Tears were spilling onto her cheeks. "If you're not back by when, five minutes…ten minutes? I'm not leaving you."

"Give me twenty minutes. Okay? Anna, okay?" She shook her head.

"I'll be okay," I whispered. I hugged her and turned toward the pool of water.

"And what if some of the kids from school come out here early just as we did? I'm not hiding back there like some scared child," she protested.

"Anna, get behind the falls." I slid into the water.

The silence of the water filled my ears as I swam toward the bottom. It was much warmer than it had been before. Its warmth comforted me I swam downward toward the tunnel that leads into the cavern. I swam and pulled my way through the fully submerged tunnel. The water temperature changed; it felt cold. The shaft suddenly made a sharp turn upward. I found myself in a narrow cylinder of rock. I pulled my way upward, not knowing where it was leading or if it would be a dead-end.

Something seemed different. The water sounded different. It was the sound that water makes as it is being drained, a gurgling sound almost. Instantly, I was being pulled down, back toward the opening that leads into the waterfall pool. It was as though I was caught in a whirlpool of some kind. Water swirled and churned all around me. I had no control of my body as it spun. My mind couldn't focus. My lungs began to burn, needing air. Then just as quickly as it had started...it stopped. The water began to calm. My vapor-like body moved upward again, through the narrow tunnel, turning and twisting through the rocky passageway.

Suddenly, I broke the surface. As my eyes cleared, I found myself in a dimly lit cave. I pulled myself up out of the tight crevice as my body began to take back its form. I stood on the rocky ledge, looking around. It seemed to be a small area; a damp and musty smell filled the air. The roar of the falls was deafening. Through the darkness, there were glimmers of light shining through cracks in the rock walls that loomed high above me. I stepped carefully along the slippery surface, taking in the space that surrounded me. About twenty feet or so up the rock wall, there was an opening. *Another cave?* I wondered. Water was streaming down the sides of the slick, mossy rocks, pooling all around. The wet stones glistened as the rays bounced off them.

I made my way closer to the wall, carefully stepping from rock to rock, beginning to see a little more clearly. The cavern seemed to go deeper inside this rock tomb. I felt my way around the inside wall, it seemed to circle within itself. It got darker and darker as I inched farther away from the only light source: the light that was streaming through the crevice in the rocks from the sun that was shining brightly outside this stone dungeon that was under the waterfall.

The smell hit me as I rounded the curvature in the cavern wall. I covered my nose and mouth with one hand and felt my way along the wall with the other. Suddenly, I slipped, putting my hands down to break my fall. Feeling around to steady myself, my hand touched something that felt like hair...human hair. The stench took my breath as it filled the air. I turned to look at the body that was lying next to me, what was left of it. I knew who it was. It was the guy from one of the photos, the one that was missing. He was the piece of the puzzle that I had not thought about yet.

Suddenly, it all began to make sense. I slid across the rocks to the opposite wall. My body heaved as I threw up.

"You came," I heard her say. "I knew you would."

I sprang to my feet and leaned back against the wall. I stayed silent and motionless.

"I see you found one of the shells. Why don't you come out and see my next one?"

It was Sariai.

"Don't make me take her," she hissed. I heard a faint moan. "Not before I get the pleasure of seeing you look into her eyes and not be able to do a thing about it."

The moans had turned to sobs. I slowly made my way around the wall of the cave toward the sound of her voice.

They were standing there, the light surrounded their silhouettes against the darkness of the cave. Anna was there beside her, struggling to keep her balance. A handful of her hair was wound tightly in Sariai's hand. She yanked her head back. Fear and pain gripped Anna's face.

"I'm sorry," Anna cried. Tears mixed with water dripped down her face.

"Sorry? Don't be sorry. This is going even better than I had hoped," she smirked. Again pulling Anna's head back by her hair.

"Let her go!" I shouted. "It's me you want...not her."

"Neither one of you are going anywhere," she shoved Anna toward me.

I tried to catch her. We both fell back into the cold water that had filled one of the small pools inside the cave.

I quickly got to my feet, never taking my eyes off Sariai. "Anna, get behind me." She lay there in the shallow pool with only her face up out of the water. "Anna, get up!" Sariai was inching toward us.

"I can't move," she murmured. "I think my leg is broken." I bent down beside Anna, looking at her broken leg.

"Look out," Anna screamed, shoving me over on my side. The blow hit her. The crack echoed as the rock struck the side of her head.

Before I could react, Sariai was on top of me, holding me down, forcing my head under the water. I could see her face through the flowing water that was coming from above us, a waterfall within the cave. I didn't struggle. I just stared into her hollow dark eyes. I knew my body was changing; I could feel it. The difference this time was that I welcomed it. I wanted it. I was willing it. Her body was changing too. Water had the same effect on both of us. I heard a moan from Anna. She was still alive.

You have the power within you. It was not Ben's voice I was hearing. It was my own. I threw her off me. She landed across the cave. I was on my feet and moving toward her as if they were not even beneath me. I pinned her against the wall of the cave. Her eyes turned red, and in an instant, she moved through me. I felt a burning sensation like my body was on fire. She whirled around and shoved my face into the jagged edge of one of the rocks. I felt the warmth of blood as it oozed down my face. The incredible heat I felt was unbearable. She was pressing herself into me. I felt nauseous; dizziness came over me. It was like the energy within my being was being sucked out.

You have the power to fight her... Believe in yourself, I thought. Even as my body became weaker and weaker.

"You think you can defeat me? You don't have half the power that I do." She threw me across the cavern like I was a ragdoll. My body—half-human, half-vapor—slammed against the rocks that dotted the floor. I lay there face up, limp in the pool of water.

She knelt over me. "You were mine that day at the airport. Do you think Ion wants you? He doesn't want you. He chose you for me."

I heard her words. I tried to make sense of it, but my mind was spinning. *Ion.* She had used that name when I heard her talking with Liam. It was the name that the one Ben referred to as Father had called him that night. That night in the water when the fate of so many was at stake. *Just like now*, I thought.

My fingers felt the large rock under my right hand. With one stunning blow, I smashed it against her head. She fell lifelessly on top of me. Her vapor-like form instantly became fully human. I pushed her off me; her body rolled onto her back. I stared at the soft, pretty features of the girl named Audrey as she lay there in the shallow water. She looked so innocent.

Anna! I thought. I crawled over to where she lay. "Anna," I said softly, touching her face.

"You are an angel, aren't you?" She smiled up at me.

Chapter Thirteen

A beam of light from the crack between the rocks was shining directly on me. I looked down at my body as Anna reached out to touch me. The light was illuminating my half vapor-like body. The coolness of the air filled the cave. The warmth from the brilliant beam was casting a halolike glow around me. Her hand reached for mine. I felt the heat of her touch. I thought of that night on the beach with Ben, how it felt to have been able to feel his heartbeat. I took her hand in mine and reached out with my other hand to gently touch the gash on the side of her head. It began to glow as the wound closed and healed instantly.

"Are you okay?" I asked.

"Sure," Anna said. "Other than I can't feel my leg, and my head is throbbing." She moaned as she felt the side of her head.

"Come on, we have to get you out of here," I put my arm under hers and lifted her up out of the pool of water. We stood there as she leaned against me trying to get her balance, not able to put any weight on her leg. I glanced over at Sariai. Her body was lying there…eerily still.

"She killed him, Christi," Anna whispered.

"What? Who?" I looked back at her.

"Liam, she killed him! They came to the waterfall. First, it was Liam. I know I was supposed to stay hidden, but…but I thought it was just Liam, so I came out. He and I were talking—when she showed up and they, they began to argue." She was talking too fast, stumbling over her words. "They were arguing about me. I think he was trying to protect me somehow. It was Liam, but he didn't sound like Liam. His voice was different. She called him something else, not Liam. Then…then she did something to him. I don't know, it was like my eyes blurred—then he just collapsed. They were arguing about me, and she killed him." She was sobbing.

"Anna, slow down." I took her by the shoulders and shook her. "You do not know that. He could still be alive. We need to get you out of here." I wanted her to focus. Her face was pale, and she looked like she was about to pass out.

"How? I can't even stand up," she moaned, staring blankly at me.

She was right. She couldn't on her own, not with her leg like it was. I needed to do something. I was responsible for her even being here. She was in danger because of me. "Here, let's move over there," I said, nodding toward the other side of the pool of water.

I helped her as she hobbled a few feet, then carefully sat down on the rocks. She looked so innocent sitting there. Her face had streaks of dried blood down the side of her cheek. I looked down at her shattered leg that was red and swollen. Kneeling beside her, I reached out, and I placed my hands on her leg. I could feel the heat that flowed through my arm down to my hands and through my fingertips. An overwhelming warmth that radiated from my touch to her skin.

"What's happening?" She leaned back on her hands, looking on in amazement.

Her leg began to glow under my hands.

"Just like the wolf," she whispered.

"Come on, we have to hurry." I stood and walked over to the small pool of water where we had entered into the cavern. She sat there, looking at her leg, letting what had just happened sink in. "Anna!" She slowly got up and walked over to where I was standing. We looked at our reflections in the dark pool of water below us.

Suddenly, there was a noise behind us. "Where is she? She's gone," Anna said as she looked at the spot where Sariai had been.

My eyes darted up and down, looking for any sign of movement in the blackness that surrounded the outer walls of the cave.

"Don't fool yourself. Don't think he's coming to help you." The sound of her voice came from above us. She was there in the opening in the cave wall, twenty feet up. "Soon, I will have all the power I need. Not even Ion will be able to stop me. Do you wonder where he is? Why he has not come to save you?" She was taunting me. "You think he loves you. He doesn't care about you. Besides, he'll be mine soon. He has no idea what I am capable of. Run along now," she gestured, dismissively waving her hand at us. "Exciting things are coming. It's going to be a blast," she laughed as she spoke. Then she disappeared through the opening.

"What is she talking about? Who's Ion? Did she mean Liam?" Anna was looking at me for answers.

"I think there is an underground entrance to the old power plant through a tunnel here in the cave. That tunnel." I looked at the dark opening.

"Oh my god! The power plant, what does that mean?" The panic was evident in her voice.

"Now, listen, you need to hold your breath, just like you did when she pulled you in here."

"I can't, I can't hold my breath that long again, I can't do it," she cried.

"Yes, you can. You have to," I reached for her, holding her face in my hands, making her look at me. "You take a deep breath and then feel your way back through the tunnel. At the end of the tunnel, where it turns…if you feel like you are in some sort of whirlpool, don't panic, don't fight against it…just wait…it will stop. You're almost there, keep going, you will come out in the waterfall pool."

She was shaking. "What?" Her eyes were darting back and forth.

"Anna, are you listening?" I still held her face in my hands, looking her in the eyes. "First you need to check on Liam, and then go get help. Tell Aunt Abby to call that detective. Tell her to tell him something is going to happen at the old power plant. That the missing girl is there." Her eyes were darting from me to the opening in the cave wall above us, then back to the water tunnel beneath us.

"Look at me," I said to her. "Don't worry about me. I'll be fine," I tried to reassure her. "And another thing, you have to promise me not to talk about what just happened here. Not to anyone."

"I don't even know what happened here." Tears were spilling onto her cheeks. "How could I explain it to anyone, especially to that detective? He can't know I'm involved, Christi."

"What are you talking about? None of this is your fault." She was silent. "You can't be blamed for any of this," I was getting impatient. "Talk to me." Time was running out.

"My dad and I are illegal, the girl at school was right. Mr. Tom has been working on fixing it with my dad. If I talk to them, if they get involved, they'll know." I could hear the fear in her voice.

"Listen to me, we can't worry about that right now. This is extremely important, Anna, this is about more than you or me."

She looked at me. "What are you going to do?"

"I don't know, but I have to try to stop her before anyone else gets hurt." I thought of the body that was lying just a few yards away from us. "And there's more. You need to tell them the body of that missing guy is here…in this cave."

"Oh my god!" Her body swayed, she grabbed my arm to steady herself. "Is that who she was talking about? Is that Ion?"

I grabbed her by the shoulders. "No…there's nothing we can do for this guy now, but maybe we can help Liam. You need to focus on what I'm saying. You hear me?" She shook her head and wiped her face with her hand. "Now, you need to go." She leaned forward and hugged me. "It'll be okay. We'll be okay."

A tear ran down her cheek as she sat down on the watery opening into the cave. Just before she slipped into the dark water, she looked up at me. "Promise?" she whispered. She took a deep breath and disappeared into its blackness.

Now what? I stood there, feeling confused and helpless. Not knowing what I was going to do next or what was about to happen. Worried about Anna, and yet knowing I did not have time to think about her. I stared at the opening where Sariai had gone. *How could I possibly be able to follow her?*

I looked at the pool of water. I had always tried to suppress the effects that it had on my body. I knew how it would change. But I also knew that as soon as I was out of the water, I would begin to change back. It wouldn't be long enough to catch up with her.

You can control it. Ben had told me that. I closed my eyes. *Was he preparing me for this?* I concentrated on my body. I visualized it from my head to my toes. Every inch of it. Then, just as quickly, I pictured myself as a vapor, floating in the air. Floating up…just like a mist would rise above the water.

My mind drifted back to all those months ago. The night Ben had carried me out of the water. *You are stronger than you even know. You're a fighter.* Ben had said, softly stroking my hand. I saw myself lying in a hospital bed. I looked around the room. IV bags on stands and monitors made an occasional beep. There was a tube that led to my wrist. I could hear the hum of the fluorescent lights that hung from the ceiling. Aunt Abby was sleeping in a chair that had been shoved into a corner of the tiny room.

"Ben?"

"Shhh," he said softly. "You are going to be fine. Stronger than ever."

I felt the same burning sensation that ran the length of my arm into my very core. I was dizzy. I tried to focus on the tube that was dripping liquid into the vein in my wrist. My eyes ran the length of the long, clear tube. The other end was not attached to the bag that hung from the IV stand. It was connected to Ben.

"*Christi!*" The sound of his voice jolted my conscience. Opening my eyes, I found myself suspended in mid-air at the opening of the tunnel.

Through its rocky formation, I glided. Moving through the darkness as a fish moves through the water. Around rocks and through water-filled crevices. I knew what was ahead of me. Both inside the tunnel, and what I would find at the end. I was ready for it.

The damp rocky tunnel lead into what appeared to be a concrete bunker of some kind. Some lights hung from the ceiling that had long since burned out. I reached up and touched one of the rusted fixtures. Suddenly it lit up, and its dim beam began to light up the square concrete room that I found myself in. My body was starting to slip back into its human form.

Along one of the walls, there were metal rungs embedded in the concrete like a ladder. It ran upward to an opening where a metal cover had been slid to the side. *This is it*, I thought and began to climb the rungs.

I pulled myself out of the circular opening into a hall-way. A stairway was to the left and on the right were rusted metal cages that contained some sort of huge fans. I was in the basement of the power plant. I knew that I needed to find her before it was too late. I began to make my way up the flight of stairs. *She could be anywhere,* I thought as I climbed another flight. Stopping somewhere between floors, I closed my eyes, and listened. At first, I heard nothing. Then…a faint closing of a metal door. *She was close.* I moved upward, another floor closer to the sound.

It was the big yellow rectangle sign on the double doors in front of me that stopped me. A symbol of purple fan blades with lettering that spelled out "Danger Radioactive Material." It froze me in my tracks. Even though I knew inside what she was capable of, it suddenly sunk in. Fear bombarded my mind. Thoughts of what she might be planning flashed through my mind like a movie on fast forward. Aunt Abby, my mom, Poppie, Anna…

"Stop it!" I shouted. *Concentrate. Dammit!* I could not face Sariai in the half-human form that I was in.

Suddenly, the doors flung open; she was standing there just a few feet away.

"Good, you made it," she smirked. "I was counting on it," she laughed. She lunged forward, pinning me against the concrete wall of the stairwell. I had not been fast enough. I felt the warm blood running down the back of my head.

"Don't worry. I'm not going to kill you now. No, I want you alive just long enough to see what power I have." Her face was inches from mine. "You think I needed you?" She snarled. "I don't need anyone now." She released her grip on me as my body slid down the wall leaving a streak of blood on its dull white finish. "I could absorb the life out of you just like that." She snapped her fingers as she stooped down and put her hand on my head. The pain was like fire. My head felt like it would explode. I was powerless against her.

"But no, not yet." She abruptly stood.

"Get up!" she commanded.

The burning pain subsided, as my body seemed to rise on its own without any effort from me. I stood there, leaning against the wall. I tried to stay conscious and focus my eyes on her.

She reached out, grabbed my hair, and began pulling me up the stairs. The pain in my head again was numbing. She pushed open the large metal door, dragging me as we exited the building onto a walkway.

It was the same walkway Aunt Abby and I had seen earlier. The one Detective Baker had been on. It ran the length of the dam. Half running, stumbling, she dragged me across the metal grating. She stopped about halfway across.

"You see that?" She forced me upward, straightened my body. "Way out there." She was pointing out across the dam. "See those little tiny buildings? The ones with their tiny metal roofs shining in the sunlight. That's your family's place." She smirked. "And the home of that worthless, coward of a shell...Liam." She yanked my head around so I would face her. "And beyond that is the school, the whole town. You thought you could stop me?" Her hot breath was inches from my face. "Well, look at you now." She laughed. "You are going to stand here and watch. Watch as I destroy this whole place. Knowing that what the flood water from the dam does not destroy, the effects of the radiation will." She seemed to be enjoying every second of telling me her plan. "It'll not only kill now but for years to come. I'll be famous, and that's only the beginning." She forced me to my knees. "You want to know what the best part of this is going to be. You can't do anything to stop it."

"No...but, I can!"

Our backs were to the sound of his voice. We both knew who it was...it was Ben. I could see her body stiffen. She pulled me to my feet, tightening my body against hers. In an instant, she whirled my body around, never loosening her grip on me. We stood there facing him.

"Let her go, Sariai. This has nothing to do with her. This is between you and me." His voice was calm.

"You're wrong Ion, this is all about her. Or should I call you Ben, after all, you are not Ion anymore, are you?" Her voice was filled with bitterness. "The problems between you and me all started with her. What about the night you chose her for me? Don't you remember that?" She tightened the grip that she had on my hair. "Of course you do. I think she should hear all about it."

I was helpless; my knees felt weak as I stood there looking into his eyes.

"Let's tell her all about the plan, the plan that we had—how it was supposed to be, Ion. You and me. We were going to start a whole new life for us here...for all of us." She started to back across the walkway, pulling me with her. "Now, they are all gone. Dead, Ion! For what? Her?" she screamed at him, yanking my head back.

"Let her go, then we can talk about it." He was talking to her, but he never took his eyes off me.

"Why would I do that?" she snarled. "You know I can take her. I have the power now to take out this whole place, just like that." She pulled me even tighter against her body. I felt like I couldn't breathe.

"She's stronger than you think, Sariai. Besides, she has fate on her side." He was calm, and there was a gentleness as he spoke. "Listen to me. You don't have the power you think you do. The radiation here has been inactive for years. It has no effect on you. You get no power from it. In fact, it's just the opposite. It's destroying what power you have." He kept talking, inching closer to us.

"That's not true, you're lying to me." She stopped. "Darius studied it. He did the research on the human's computer and reported back to me." She shook her head in confusion.

I could feel the power in her body begin to fade. And mine began to respond. My head was starting to clear, and my eyes began to focus.

"He lied to you, Sariai. He was in it for himself. You know how he is. He has always wanted power. Father warned us, don't you remember?" He was still moving ever so slightly toward us. "He wanted you to think that, so he could take your power from you." He was just a few feet away from us now. "And where is he now? Why isn't he here with you? Helping you carry out this plan of yours? Doesn't that tell you something?"

"I knew he was keeping something from me. I thought he was trying to protect that human girl…her…over me. Just like you are doing right now, for her," she hissed. "Choosing this one over me." She dragged me further across the walkway as she spat her words at him.

My eyes were on Ben; I could see the sense of helplessness in his eyes. Not being able to free me from her grasp from his will alone.

"I thought it was his interest in that human that was weakening him. He was betraying me the whole time." Her voice broke as emotion shook her body.

Her grip on me loosened slightly. I thought of Liam and what Anna said had happened as I listened to her. Not knowing if the words that Ben was speaking to her was the truth or not. If he knew what had happened to Liam, or if he was just trying to distract her. Either way, it was working. I could feel my body strengthening.

"We can still make this work, Sariai," he said softly. "You and I, just like we planned. But you need to let her go."

"Why her, Ion? Why not me?" Her grip on me again loosened as sadness overwhelmed her. "I can't live in the same world as her. Knowing you chose her instead of me." Her body shook as she tried to make sense of what he was telling her. I could feel the emotion in her body; her heart raced as she pressed my body tighter against hers. "I should have eliminated them all at the waterfall. Darius, that human girl, and this one."

If I was going to have any chance, it was now. *You can do it*, I heard his voice within my soul.

"Her name is Anna," I said as my body began to instantly change. I pushed against her. She stumbled backward, taking a handful of my hair as she fell.

I felt it as her hand slid down my arm, and she grabbed for my wrist. Just a slight snag. I caught a glimpse of it as it fell between the metal gratings of the walkway. I heard the faint tinkling sound it made as it hit against the metal. The sun reflected off its gold chain. My bracelet.

Instantly, Ben was there; he quickly pushed me behind him and stood over her. My exhausted body sank onto the thin metal grating of the walkway. She sat there on the grating looking up at him. I tried to focus on them, listening to what they were saying over the roar of the water as it spilled over the dam.

"What choice are you going to make, Ion?" Her eyes darted back and forth, her body twitched like a caged animal. Suddenly, she rolled over to the side and through the opening of the walkway railing. Just as quickly, Ben dove forward, catching her by the hand as her body fell through the opening. She struggled, trying to free herself of his hold on her.

"Either you destroy me now...or let me go," she said. "Which decision can you live with, Ion?"

He lay there on the metal grating as she dangled in his grip. "You know I can't let you hurt anyone else." His voice softened.

"But you can destroy me?" she cried. "I love you, Ion. I've always loved you." I watched them, the torment reflected on their faces as they looked into each other's eyes.

It seemed like minutes past before she spoke. "Then do it, Ion...I'd rather not exist than to exist without you." Tears were running down her face.

I sat there. Watching as their bodies became vapor. They appeared exactly the same, two round balls of light that seemed to melt into one another. There was no resistance. I couldn't detect one from the other in the vapor-like mist. It was over quickly. Ben was standing there as the mist cleared. He was holding the limp body of the girl named Audrey. He gently laid her onto the walkway and turned to look at me. I felt sick. Sick from all that had happened. All that could have happened.

The sound of sirens broke the silence.

"No matter what happens now," he said, walking toward me, "don't ever doubt how special you are."

I leaned my head back against the railing as the light turned into darkness.

Chapter Fourteen

I sat there on the porch swing, tying my shoes. Looking out at the mountains, I patiently waited for Aunt Abby to bring out our morning coffee.

Everything that had happened the day before was flashing through my mind. Playing like a movie on fast-forward. Closing my eyes, I tried to sort out the events in my mind. I envisioned the lights from the emergency vehicles that had responded to the power plant. The sound of the fire engines sirens as their screams echoed through the valley. I sat on the back bumper of the ambulance as the EMTs wheeled a gurney past me. A sheet covered the body of the teenage girl named Audrey. Her long blond hair flowed from under the white sheet.

Now, I sat here on this porch swing, the morning sun warming on my face. Tears rolled down my cheek as I thought of these two innocent people who had gotten caught up in something beyond their control. Something they had been powerless against. Three really, there was Liam.

I had not seen Ben since being with him on the walkway. I had looked around for him. I asked about him. No one had any answers.

My mom and Aunt Abby had been at the hospital when the ambulance that carried me arrived. After a few hours of blood work and monitoring, *I had a concussion, the nausea was from that,* they had told us. After a few hours of "being observed," I was released to go home. *To rest.* I was fine…it was the fate of everyone else that I was worried about.

Detective Baker had stopped by my room to question me. *Formalities,* he had said. I lied as I told him I couldn't remember what had happened. That I remembered going to the waterfall with Anna, but nothing after that.

That's enough for now, my mom had insisted. *She needs to rest.*

There will be time for more details and questions later, Detective Baker had said.

Aunt Abby had filled me in about Anna. She had told them that Liam and the girl that was missing, had come to the waterfall after we had gotten there. That they began to argue. They were talking about some plan that she had and that he had tried to stop her. They confronted each other, and then all of a sudden, Liam collapsed. She thought maybe he had had a heart attack. Anna had told her that the missing girl and I had struggled. That she had forced me to go with her to the old power plant. Leaving her there with Liam. She had somehow managed to get Liam onto Midnight, and they had made their way back to the Bakers.

Thank God his dad was home, Aunt Abby had said.

We had stopped by Liam's room before we left the hospital.

It's his heart, his mom told us. *It's out of rhythm, but they are hopeful that he was going to be okay. He had not yet regained consciousness. They're waiting for him to wake up before they run any more tests. So thankful for Anna, she saved his life.* His dad was sitting silently at his son's bedside, holding his hand. *How did he get involved with this girl? On the internet? They are calling her a terrorist.* Her voice shook, the worry showing in her face. *They came and took his computer from the house. Thank goodness John's brother is on the case. He knows Liam wouldn't get involved in something like this. There has to be an explanation. I just want him to wake up.* She cried as we stood there, just inside the door.

My mom hugged her, trying to encourage her that it was going to be okay.

Then we stopped by Anna's room; her dad was sitting with her. Flowers and balloons filled her room. Notes had been taped to her bedside table. *Some of the kids from school brought them,* Manny had said.

I stood beside her bed and read them.

You are so brave. Thank you, Anna. You're a hero! another note read. I touched her hand as she lay there sleeping. The doctors said she too had a concussion. She was dehydrated and running a high fever, but she was going to be okay.

I wiped a tear from my chin as I thought of the danger I had put her in. The lies she was forced to tell because of me. But *this...*I remember thinking as I read the notes. *She deserves this.*

What about Ben? I had kept asking them. They knew no other details about Ben after we were taken from the scene. *Please! Find out something,* I had pleaded with them.

We will, honey, my mom had said. *Right now, we need to get you home so you can rest.*

I did sleep when we got home. And for the first time in a very long time, it was not interrupted by dreams.

Sitting here now, I wondered if I will ever really rest again. Not when everything that had happened kept racing through my mind. The danger from Sariai was over, but now I had more questions.

I couldn't wait to go to the hospital to see Anna this morning. She would be disappointed that Liam did not get to have the party at the waterfall. She was so looking forward to it. There will be plenty of time for that. The important thing now was…she was going to be *okay*…she had to be.

I sat there soaking in the morning light. Everything seemed so normal. The birds were chirping, looking for their breakfast. There was a slight breeze that rustled the leaves on the trees. I could hear the horses moving restlessly in the barn.

"Here we are, Luvy," Aunt Abby came through the screen door carrying two cups of coffee. "With two sugars, with a lot of our favorite creamer…just like we like it." She handed me a cup as she sat down on the swing beside me. "Your mom's on the phone with Tom. He and Poppie will be on their way home soon. She'll join us for coffee when she's finished." She patted my leg.

"I am so thankful for my family, especially for you, Aunt Abby. I don't know what I would do if anything happened to you." The thought of what could have happened sent a shiver down my spine. I took a sip of the warm coffee, pulling my sweatshirt tighter around my body.

"Oh, Luvy, nothing in this life is guaranteed. We have to get up each day and try to live it to its fullest." She sipped her coffee. "Loving God first, then ourselves and others. Just like He loves us. But..." She grinned and nudged me with her shoulder. "I plan to live a long, happy life. I want to see you go to college, get married, have kids. So I can spoil them, just like I've always spoiled you." She paused. "Your mom, though, she says she's afraid to leave the two of us alone anymore. It seems strange things happen when it's just the two of us. I think she may be right," she mused, looking serious for a moment. Then she laughed, making a waving motion with her hand.

"Did you know that Anna and her dad are not US citizens?"

She looked at me for a moment before she answered. "Yes, but where in the world did that come from? Your mom was telling me about it. But she also said that Tom is working with Manny to get their paperwork submitted. And something tells me, after what Anna did yesterday, how brave she was, how brave you both were, Detective Baker will do all he can to start the process even sooner."

"Do you think I talk weird?" My mind was flitting from one thing to another. I shifted my weight in the swing so I could see her face as she responded.

"What are you talking about?" She laughed, almost choking on her coffee. "Are you okay? Is this your concussion talking?"

"I am serious. I am not trying to be funny." I stopped the swing and looked at her. "Do you think I talk funny?"

"Do you mean ha-ha funny?" she asked, her laugh stopped mid-chuckle. "No, you do not talk funny, not any more than I do." She was stern with seriousness in her tone.

"That really does not answer my question, Aunt Abby. Maybe we both talk weird."

"Oh, Luvy, we love each other so much. Who cares if we use bad grammar from time to time?" She put her arm around me. "What's going on? Did someone say something to you?"

"It doesn't matter," I whispered. Suddenly wondering why I was even letting it bother me. How unimportant it was.

She paused for a moment, shrugged, and using her best southern accent, she said, "Well, we do say…tater chip." She winked at me, as we burst out laughing.

"Your dad will get in this morning," my mom said, opening the screen door and stepping onto the porch. "What's so funny?" she asked.

"Oh, nothing. Just a little morning humor," Aunt Abby answered.

"Why did you call him? He'll only worry. I am fine. He did not need to fly all the way out here," I sighed.

"I know, honey, he's your dad. You had to know he would want to come and see for himself."

"But I am coming home in a few days anyway," I stood and walked over to the railing that ran the length of the porch. "Everybody worries too much," I whispered.

"Because we love you," she said softly.

I looked down at my wrist. It seemed so bare. It felt like a part of me was missing. *How can I tell my mom I had lost it?*

"Is that Tom and Poppie?" she asked, looking down the drive.

We turned to see the car coming up the gravel driveway. The sound of the tires crunching against the stone scattered the birds that were searching for worms in the middle of it. It stopped in front of the house. It was Detective Baker.

"Good morning, ladies." He came around the front of the vehicle.

"Good morning," Aunt Abby responded as she got up from the swing and walked down the steps to greet him.

"How's she doing this morning?" he looked up at me as I made my way to the top of the steps.

"*She*...is doing fine," I answered.

"You're not here to question her again now, are you? Can't this wait?" my mom asked, standing beside me.

"How's Ben? Where is he? Is he okay?" The questions were pouring out of my mouth.

He stood there for a moment, looking up at me. "Why don't you ask him yourself," he said, walking to the back door of his car. He opened it. Ben stepped out.

Tears began to fill my eyes as I made my way down the steps. Slowly, taking each step, afraid that if I took my eyes off him, he might disappear when I stepped on the next one.

He reached out to take my hand. "Take a walk with me. If that's okay?" He looked at my mom, then to Detective Baker.

"I'm not sure that I'm okay with that," my mom answered. I turned to glare at her. "I mean it," she continued. "Everything that has happened to you, he has been involved some way."

"Let her go, Joni, she'll be all right. Maybe we do worry too much," Aunt Abby said to her as she walked over and hugged me. She took the coffee cup from my hand, then turned to hug Ben. "Thank you," she whispered to him.

"She's right, Mrs. Snyder, you don't need to worry. She'll be fine," Detective Baker said.

I looked back at my mom and Aunt Abby as I put my hand in his. My mom didn't say anything; she just nodded in agreement.

Together we walked down the drive. I cupped his hand in both of mine. I turned to face him, walking backward… looking at him. It felt good to just look at him…to be with him without the sense of fear hanging over us.

"Ben, what happened?"

"Shhh, no questions. Let's just walk for a while."

We walked onto the main road. We did what he asked. We didn't talk; we just walked. Taking in the surroundings and each other. The mountain ranges that were so beautiful and peaceful in the morning light. A fog hung over the low-lying areas in the distance. But mostly…just looking at each other.

"You know, I am a runner," I finally broke the silence, letting go of his hand. "Technically, that was a statement, not a question." I was defending the fact that I was speaking. He smiled.

"Can you keep up with me?" I asked as I ran ahead of him. "Are you coming?" I looked back.

"Just giving you a head start, Princess," he yelled.

"Oh! You did not just call me that!" I stopped and began to walk back toward him.

"First to the train tracks," he laughed as he flew past me.

"Moron," I whispered, smiling.

We were nearing the culvert where the wolf had been trapped when his pace began to slow.

"What's the matter? Giving up already?" I yelled sarcastically.

"We have a curious onlooker." He nodded toward the grassy field to our left. "See him? There, about twenty yards out."

I did see him. His reddish gray fur moving silently through the thick grass. "This is not our first meeting. It seems our paths are destined to cross," I mused.

"That sounds mysterious and a story I'd like to hear. But first, we have a race to finish." He took off, leaving me standing there.

"No fair, you distracted me," I yelled at him.

I looked in the direction of the wolf. He was still there, his green eyes fixed on me as if he was waiting for me to move. *What is going on with you?* I thought. I looked for any sign of the other two. He was alone.

All of a sudden, I felt sick. Leaning forward, I put my hands on my knees. My insides seemed to be on fire as my body shook, and beads of sweat ran down my face. I had felt it before, but this time, it was different. *Don't throw up...don't throw up*, I whispered to myself.

I slowly turned; the wolf was gone.

This is what you have been waiting for, I thought. Straightening my body, I tried to focus on what was ahead. *You can do this.*

Ben was waiting for me at the *T.* "What took you so long?" he teased. Smiling, he wrapped his arms around me.

I wanted us to stand like that forever. I felt safe in his arms, thankful, praying that this feeling of security and belonging would never end.

A train whistled in the distance.

"Ever wanted to jump on a train?" I looked up at him.

"No, have you?" His forehead wrinkled with furrows that creased his skin.

"Yes, let's do it! Fully human, though. No fancy stuff." I pulled on his arm, dragging him backward, away from the intersection.

"Seriously?" He stood there, staring at me in disbelief. "Just jump on a train? And ride it where?"

"Just into town. You have to time it just right though," I answered.

The sound of the train's wheels, metal against metal, rang out in the morning air. The train was getting closer and closer. The tracks were just a few yards from us. We could hear the rattle of the cars as they rocked back and forth. This time I was going to do it.

He knew I was serious. "Okay." He took my hand. "We do this together."

We stood there waiting. Waiting for the perfect time.

"Now!" I shouted as the first few cars passed and the one whose open door was just a few car lengths away.

We ran together, stride for stride across the asphalt pavement, up and over the small embankment. Suddenly we were flying in the air. Screaming like little kids as we landed on the floor inside the open doors of the railcar, rolling to a stop on the other side.

"We did it!" I exclaimed as I took a breath, sliding back against the side wall of the boxcar.

"Yes, we did." He pulled himself beside me and leaned his head back against the metal wall. My heart was pounding in my chest.

We sat there catching our breath, looking at the empty car that had been the transport for animals. The sides were slated for air to get in. It had the smell of horses. It was a smell that I loved. There was straw scattered around in the corners where the wind had whirled it into piles.

Suddenly, a movement caught our eyes at the same time. We looked at each other in disbelief. I looked where he had gracefully landed, just feet from us. He shook his massive body, walked over to one of the opposite corners, and laid down in the straw as if it were his bed. *Why shouldn't I believe it?* I wondered. *After all that had happened.*

"Wow, you weren't kidding. You really have made a friend, haven't you?

We looked in amazement and disbelief, as he lay there just a few feet away, licking his body, relaxing as if he too hopped onto a train every day.

"Have you given him a name yet? It is a he, isn't it?" We stared at the beautiful creature that had begun to groom himself. "I think you should name him Sam," he said.

I thought about Mrs. Jackson…she would be pleased.

"Animals can sense kindness, you know. I guess you have a way with them, just like you have with me," he whispered.

"Hum, maybe so." I smiled.

"Maybe…there's more to you than I thought." He put his arm around me as I laid my head back against his chest.

"And there is still so much more about you that I need to know." I intertwined my fingers in his.

"You know the important stuff. Isn't that enough?" He lifted my hand to his lips and kissed it gently.

"I'm serious!" I turned my body to face him, sitting crossed legged as I leaned forward and kissed him on the cheek.

"What do you want to know?" he asked.

"I want to know where you have been. What you have been doing. I want to know what Sariai meant when she said that you chose me for her."

He ignored my questions as he leaned forward, took my face in his hands, and brushed his lips lightly against mine.

"I want to know everything about you. From the beginning," I whispered.

"You are my beginning." He kissed me again.

"Why does my stomach feel like there are a million butterflies in it, and my head spins every time you do that?" He leaned back, pulling me onto his chest.

I lay there with my head against him. I could feel his heartbeat under my chin. I ran my hand down the length of his arm and clasp my fingers around his hand.

Across the wooden floor, Sam slept peacefully.

The boxcar rocked back and forth in a soothing motion. And if I let my mind wander just enough…the noise that the wheels made against the tracks almost sounded like music.

It was enough… For now.

Acknowledgments

This book is a result of support and encouragement from so many people, without which, this story would have gone untold.

I want to say a special thank you to Debbie Sparks for allowing me the privilege of not only sharing the story within the pages of my book but, more importantly, the personal story that's forever written in my heart.

To Kelly Crum at Page Publishing, thank you for your patience when I was sometimes overanxious. You have been a ray of sunshine during this process.

To my family and friends, thank you for proofreading, editing, critiquing, praising, and for always encouraging me to pursue my writing. You exemplify that it's not *blood* that makes you family…it's *love.* If I could choose a family, I would always choose you.

To my husband, your love and understanding have been what's gotten me from day to day. You have supported me, pushed me, motivated me, and have always been the one constant in my life. Fate brought us together…you have always been my destiny.

Finally, I finish with thanking you all for reading and for helping me grow as a writer. But most of all, thank you for being a part of my journey.

With love…

About the Author

Never studied English literature, no bachelor of arts degree. Not made it to the New York Times Bestseller List…yet! Just a writer gifted with an imagination, a passion for putting together words, and a desire to tell a story.

When she was a young girl, she loved to look at the stars and imagine that she could do anything and become whatever she wanted to be…she just needed to believe in herself and keep on dreaming.

Married to her best friend and soul mate, Gail lives in beautiful Brown County in South Central Indiana. She has a fur-baby (Nala), and friends and family she adores. She's a lover of sci-fi and fantasy novels…enjoys spending time at the beach…big floppy hats…long flowy skirts… and Reese's Peanut Butter Cups.

CPSIA information can be obtained
at www.ICGtesting.com
Printed in the USA
LVHW111302190320
650567LV00001B/140

9 781646 284184